Up and down Durango Street the Gassers were looking for Rufus Henry. Not in a pack that the police might notice, but like sharks, silent and deadly. Just a few boys drifting along glancing into stores and alleys; or a boy idling on a street corner. But a single, whistled note —a telephone call from a cigar store—and the sharks would form into a pack. And Rufus Henry would have his back to the wall in an alley.

FRANK BONHAM has researched the Los Angeles-Watts area and his stories ring with the life, the language, and the toughness of a city slum. He has written many books for young readers, including *The Mystery of the Fat Cat*, *Viva Chicano*, *The Nitty Gritty*, and *Cool Cat*.

Durango Street

Street

FRANK BONHAM

LAUREL-LEAF
BOOKS

Published by
Dell Publishing Co., Inc.
1 Dag Hammarskjold Plaza
New York, New York 10017
Copyright © 1965 by Frank Bonham
All rights reserved. No part of this book
may be reproduced in any form without
permission in writing from E. P. Dutton & Co., Inc.
except by a reviewer who wishes
to quote brief passages in connection with
a review written for inclusion in a magazine,
newspaper, or broadcast. For information address
E. P. Dutton & Co., Inc., New York, New York 10003.
Laurel-Leaf Library ® TM 766734,
Dell Publishing Co., Inc.
Reprinted by arrangement with
E. P. Dutton & Co., Inc.

ISBN: 0-440-92183-X

RL: 5.8

Printed in the United States of America
First Laurel printing—August 1972
Fourteenth Laurel printing—April 1982

To George Nishi-naka,
and to the staff of Special Service for Groups

ONE

One thing the boy truly hated about the forestry camp was that there was nowhere to be alone. Absolutely nowhere. Not in the mess hall, the dormitory, nor out in the woods.

They even tried to get inside his skull.

Once a week a man named Mr. Rubio, who was a social worker, summoned Rufus to his office and they sat on opposite sides of a desk and talked. Mr. Rubio was a compact little man with a quick smile and an energetic manner. He was always rearranging things on his desk as they conversed—lining up pencils, straightening the edges of papers. He would ask questions about Rufus's mother, his father, and what he was going to do when he was released from Pine Valley Honor Camp. Often he would commence by leaning back and asking, "Well, Rufus, how are things?"

"Just fine, Mr. Rubio," Rufus would say, staring out the window. On the baseball diamond, a dozen boys might be playing ball. Others would be peeling potatoes on the steps of the mess hall. Up in the pine forest, a red slash of earth revealed where the inmates of the honor camp were building a fire road.

"Everything's just fine, Mr. Rubio," he would say.

"No problems?" Mr. Rubio would reply, as though there *had* to be problems in a detention home.

Rufus would gaze at him innocently, and shake his head. "No." Then: "How 'bout you, Mr. Rubio? You got any problems? Be glad to help you with them." And his reddish-brown features would brighten with a grin. He had a small, neat Negro head and nappy hair cut short. His features were expressive, when he was not hiding his thoughts. He wore a denim shirt and pants, bleached by many washings.

Mr. Rubio would chuckle. "I've got lots of problems, Rufus. Who hasn't? But I thought we might talk about yours."

But Rufus would never play. He had been around long enough to know that the only person who could do anything about Rufus Henry's problems was Rufus.

One day Mr. Rubio asked, "Do you remember your father, Rufus?"

"No, sir. I never saw him."

"So you can't say whether you liked him or not?"

Touched with irritation, Rufus made an impatient hand gesture. "Now, man, how would I know whether I *liked* him, if I never even *saw* him?"

"Sometimes we have impressions of things we don't actually remember."

"Well, I've got the impression that I never saw him, Mr. Rubio. That's the only impression I've got of my father."

Mr. Rubio chuckled and blew a speck of paper from his desk blotter. "I hear you're a crew leader, now," he said. "How do you like the job?"

Rufus grinned. "Fine. When I say 'frog,' those cats better jump."

Mr. Rubio wiggled a pencil reflectively. "What if a cat didn't jump?" he asked. "What would you do?"

Rufus smelled another of the sly gambits with which he was always trying to get him to explain why he had stolen and wrecked that automobile and got himself shipped to Pine Valley. But inside Rufus's mind was one place they were not going—not today, not tomorrow, not next year. So he merely shrugged and looked out the window again.

The social worker wrote something on a paper in Rufus's folder. "You haven't had many letters from your mother since you came here, it seems to me," he said thoughtfully.

"No. My old lady would rather lose a tooth than write a letter."

"Lots of people hate to write letters. I'm glad you understand that, and that your feelings aren't hurt."

Something about the statement irritated Rufus. He gazed unblinking across the desk.

"Why should my feelings be hurt?" he said. "That's stupid, letting anybody get at you that way. I've got twenty kids in my crew, and some cat's always giving me a hard time—trying to make a fool of me in front of the gang. But ol' Rufus stays on top of things. Let somebody else get his feelings hurt: I got too much to do."

Mr. Rubio nodded seriously. "Excellent philosophy," he said. "In fact—" Then he hesitated. Rufus suspected that he wanted to move quickly to another subject, but felt he must do it smoothly. He wiggled his pencil again, and finally said:

"In a way, that ability to stay on top of things is the difference between a bench-warmer and a first-string halfback. Wouldn't you say?"

In Rufus's mind a red light flashed beside the tracks. Last week, too, Mr. Rubio had mentioned football. And both times he had talked about halfbacks!

Now, that was more than coincidence.

"I guess you're right," he said calmly.

Mr. Rubio kept peering at him. Rufus's expression did not change, but inside he was angry. Baby Gibson, who had gone home a few weeks ago, had obviously told someone about Rufus's scrapbook. Rufus had over a hundred pictures of Ernie Brown, the Cleveland Corsairs' great halfback, in the book. He had collected them for years and bound them into a big loose-leaf volume with a picture of Big Ernie on the cover. Baby was the only person at camp besides Rufus who knew about his Big Ernie book. He had left it at home when he was sent to camp, knowing the headshrinkers up here would ask so many questions about it that he would have to burn the book to turn them off.

Next to having no privacy, the thing he disliked most about Pine Valley was not being able to browse through the book and talk to Ernie. He loved to study his facial expressions. When Ernie smashed through the line, his face was savage with strain and determination. Yet, sitting on the bench, his expression was oddly mild, almost perplexed. It seemed to Rufus that he was thinking:

There's a lot I don't like about this world. But it's not getting me down. I'm staying on top.

That was the way Rufus felt, too. He was staying on top.

Mr. Rubio was still watching his face. Now he said abruptly: "Rufus, I'm afraid we're going to lose you. You're going home."

Rufus started to bounce from his chair, but managed to hide his excitement. Rubbing his palms against his thighs, he asked skeptically:

"When's this going to be?"

"In a few days. The Director thinks you've made a good adjustment, that you might be better off at home."

Rufus grinned. "Isn't that exac'ly what I told the parole board three months ago?"

"Your mother's moved, by the way. Do you know the Durango Housing Project?"

"What they call the Flats? Well, I've, you know, been through it."

He had been through it one night with a dozen boys in a stolen car, shooting out store windows with a .22 rifle.

"The Flats isn't exactly an elegant part of town," Mr. Rubio said, "but your mother's managed to rent a little house. I think you'll like that better than a Project apartment. You'll have a friend in the area, by the way."

"Baby Gibson?" Rufus said. "I know. He told me he lived in the Flats."

"Walter—Baby, as you call him—can make things easier for you. He knows the area. A good friend can help there."

"He the good friend that told you about my scrapbook?" Rufus asked bluntly.

Mr. Rubio looked sheepish. "I'm sorry about that, Rufus. I didn't mean to pry. Just before Walter went home, I told him he'd be having you for a neighbor. He was tickled pink. Before he knew it, he blurted it out about a scrapbook you'd made. You see, he's a great admirer of Ernie Brown, too. And of you."

"I'm a great admirer of being told where I live before my friends get told," Rufus said pointedly.

"I didn't want you to worry, Rufus. When I was a boy, it was always a source of anxiety to me to know that I was moving. I was afraid of fights—of getting lost—all sorts of things."

Rufus knew he was supposed to confide that he too was afraid. And, in fact, he was. If gorillas had lived in Coast City, the Flats were where you'd find them screaming in the trees. His stomach had dropped the moment Mr. Rubio said, "Durango." But why tell anybody about it? Better just keep his mouth shut and see what happened.

Mr. Rubio closed Rufus's folder. "You'll be met at the bus station by a Mr. Travers. He'll be your parole officer. Let him help you, Rufus. He can, if you let him."

Rufus stood up and offered his hand, with the kind of boyish smile he thought Mr. Rubio would like.

"Thanks, Mr. Rubio," he said. "If I remember anything about my old man, I'll write you a letter."

The social worker watched him trot across the field to rejoin his work crew in the forest. Rufus traveled at an easy, loose-jointed trot, with a grace between that of a boxer and a sprinter. In his files were tests that showed that he had an excellent mind and pronounced leadership ability. But there were also remarks about gang fighting and car theft. And those were the cracks in an otherwise sound vessel that the social worker feared had not begun to mend. He sighed and slipped the folder into a drawer.

Good Luck, Rufus, he thought.

You'll need it.

TWO

A few days later, Rufus Henry was on a Greyhound bus bound for Coast City. He wore a cheap gray sport coat four inches too long, and brown slacks: gate-suits, the kids called these State-supplied outfits. As the bus traveled, nervousness grew in him. Big things were ahead, none of them very good. Going home was good; he was eager to see Curtis and Janet, his younger brother and sister.

But as he thought about the Flats, he chewed his lip. Any new neighborhood was like a cellar you entered with your hands tied behind you, the darkness brushing your face like cobwebs. Suddenly the door slammed behind you, and the darkness quaked with danger. . . .

Rufus scowled and crossed his arms. He was glad Baby Gibson lived around there. Baby was a huge, powerful boy, and he belonged to what he claimed was a strong fighting gang, the Moors. Baby should have kept his mouth shut about the scrapbook, but he was an impulsive and not very bright boy, and it must have slipped out.

Mr. Rubio could harp till he was blue in the face about staying out of gangs. But every boy at Pine Valley knew that the only way to stay alive in a big-city jungle was to join a fighting gang—before some other gang decided to use you for bayonet practice.

The bus roared out of the foothills. They passed through orange groves and pleasant suburbs. A short time later the highway splintered up in a bewildering system of freeways that dipped and swerved above one another like roller coasters. Soon the bus was skimming along on high pillars above the gray heart of the metropolis. Rufus could gaze down into the squat smokestacks of small factories.

Suddenly, like a dream of flying coming to an end, the bus swerved down an off-ramp and wedged itself into a narrow street clotted with traffic. Passengers began collecting parcels. The journey was about to end.

Rufus dragged a small carton tied with a string from under his seat. The bus squeezed into an impossibly narrow alley and halted before a cement ramp leading into the station. The engine died; there was a sigh of compressed air. As passengers clogged the exits, Rufus peered into the station, searching for the parole officer. He could make a fairly good guess as to what he would be like.

Hand on the shoulder, grin on his face. Just stay out of the gangs, boy, and you can still be President. A credit to your race. Make your father and mother real proud.

Did they really believe that stuff? Rufus wondered.

Presently, except for Rufus, the bus was empty. The driver put a metal box under his arm and prepared to leave. But seeing Rufus, he called, "End of the line, son."

For a moment Rufus did not stir. He was thinking: *Why don't I run away? Kick this town for good?* He could hitchhike to the harbor and get a job on a boat. Work his way to Africa, maybe. There was a boy in one of the gangs he'd run with that they called Watusi, because he was always talking about going to Africa, where a black boy could swing with anybody. An American Negro with a little education could easily take over a whole tribe. Be the king of the Gold Coast! Raid other tribes and steal their gold and ivory and weapons.

". . . Did you hear me?" the driver called. "This is where you get off."

Rufus stepped into the aisle. "I hear you, Chief."

He sauntered to the door. Before getting off, he paused to examine the bus schedules in a little rack. He extracted a couple and looked them over very seriously, while the driver stood there steaming. Then he stepped into the alley and walked into the station, whistling.

In the throng of people greeting friends and relatives, his eye was immediately caught by a large man in a brown suit. It was the p.o. He might as well have carried a sign that said: COP! His eyes had that quick, hunting look.

His dark butch was irregularly splashed with gray, and his heavy brows merged above his nose. His gaze locked onto Rufus and at once the officer walked forward and laid a hand on his arm.

"Rufus Henry?"

Rufus frowned at a black pearl pin in the man's tie. "That's me."

"Ed Travers." The man offered his hand. Rufus hesitated, then shifted his carton and shook hands with him. "My car's outside," the officer said. "Nice trip?"

"Uh-huh," Rufus said.

"Your mother's place is only a few minutes from here."

A blue coupe with State license plates was parked outside. As they got in, Mr. Travers picked up a folder from the seat and glanced into it.

"Man, everybody's got a folder with my name on it!" Rufus said. "When'd I get so famous?"

"About five years ago, Rufus—at least you started getting famous then. 'Gang fighting . . . runaway . . . grand theft auto . . .' "

"That auto charge—" Rufus frowned. *"No,* sir! See, these guys came by my place one night and said: 'We borrowed Andy's brother-in-law's car, man. Let's go cruising.' "

"Rufus," said the parole officer, "I can't do anything about those old charges. They're finished business. But I'll do all I can to keep you out of trouble till you've made a satisfactory adjustment back into society."

He started the engine. Rufus did not comment. Then the officer added, frankly:

"Not that I can steer anybody who doesn't want to be steered, with a case load of seventy-six boys. That gives me about three minutes a week with each boy. So I won't exactly be smothering you with attention."

Rufus liked his frankness, and also what he said. Settling into the seat, he said:

"Well, man, don't break down. I'll prob'ly get along jus' fine."

Mr. Travers started the engine. He poked the nose of the car into the traffic and drove north. Then he turned east up a street lined with small industrial plants. After a few blocks the street funneled into a narrow bridge arching above a dry riverbed. The riverbed was entirely lined with concrete. Railroad tracks filled all the flat space. On the far side, the bridge landed in a belt of small buildings. Beyond them was a long, narrow colony of angular structures in the shapes of L's and H's, all neatly fitted together like parts of a puzzle. Rufus recognized the Durango Housing Project area. The Flats.

"Kind of like to run with gangs, I hear," Mr. Travers remarked.

"Well, uh, street clubs," Rufus said.

The parole officer said: "A couple of our 'clubs' had a joint meeting the other night. One of the members was killed by an arrow with a hunting tip. Three others are in the hospital with assorted cuts and lacerations. There are over three hundred 'clubs' in the city, now, so you won't have any trouble getting lashed up with one. Except with me," he added.

"How come?" Rufus asked.

"Because one condition of your parole is that you stay unconnected, Rufus. Join a gang and I'll have to send you back to placement."

Rufus scratched his scalp. "What am I supposed to do? Join the Sea Scouts?"

"Get a job. You don't need a gang. I'll admit that if you roust any twenty kids off the sidewalk, you'll find two or three who belong to a gang. Ask them why, and they'll tell you it's for protection."

"An' that's the truth," Rufus retorted.

"What about your other eighteen boys? What do they do for protection?"

"They don't do anything, Mr. Travers. They don't need protection."

"Why not?"

"Because they won't fight. Push 'em against a wall and ask for money, and they hand it over. Tell 'em to stay away from some girl, and they drop her. Because your eighteen guys haven't got any pride, Mr. Travers. The other two or three, like me—they got pride, and they're gonna fight."

"You aren't going to fight, Rufus," replied Mr. Travers. "You're going to find a better way to handle your problems this time than breaking heads."

Rufus stared out the window, his mouth tight. *You tell me a better way, man,* he thought angrily. *Just one.*

THREE

The street—Durango Street—speared through a small, doomed area of grimy stores, restaurants, and bars. On one corner was a storefront church: The Church of the Living God. Five Negro boys stood on this corner, and Rufus felt their eyes on him and the parole officer. In one glance they knew the whole story: some kid in the custody of some cop.

Farther along was a corner taco stand with a tiny arbor squeezed between it and the brick building next door. Under the arbor, festooned with plastic ivy, were redwood picnic tables for customers. A sign on the stand said: The Happy Spot.

Mr. Travers turned into a side street in the shadow of a booming freeway that formed a solid boundary to the Flats on the east. Durango Street passed beneath the freeway and ascended a hill. But the whole Flats area was jammed between the concrete riverbed on the west and the curving gray arm of the freeway on the east.

"This is Teagarden Street," said Mr. Travers. "Your mother's place is just down the way."

Rufus scrutinized the narrow lane bordered by lettuce-green camphor trees with thin black branches. On both sides of the street were shabby houses with warped steps and porches. Many had porch railings consisting of hand-turned spindles; they looked as though they might have started out to be steamboats. He doubted whether five gallons of paint had been sold on Teagarden Street in the last twenty years. The small, dry, crumbling houses were collapsing from sheer discouragement. Even the sidewalks were worn out—lifted and cracked by tree roots. Drifts of trash were heaped between the houses, and old automobiles were being overhauled in front yards. People were sitting in chairs in front yards, watching the traffic and fanning themselves with newspapers.

Mr. Travers stopped before a house on the left, under the very arches of the freeway. "Here we are," he said cheerfully.

Rufus looked at the house. It had an upper floor consisting of a tiny room nestled under the eaves. The house gave the impression of leaning slightly to one side. A joyful melting feeling came up through him. He was home. The place everybody only had one of. Because if you had two, you really didn't have any. And if you were locked up, as he had been, then you didn't have any either, because you couldn't roam around, eat when you felt like it, or come and go without a reason and a pass.

The screen door opened. A leggy, brown-skinned girl about twelve years old came onto the porch and studied the car. She was eating an apple. She wore her hair in pigtails tied with red ribbons. Abruptly she dropped the apple and turned to shriek into the house:

"Mama! Curtis! *Rufus is home!*"

Grinning, Rufus got out and stretched. His sister, Janet, came running down the walk. She caught him in a hug, pushed her face against his coat, and began to cry. Rufus patted her on the back.

"Hey, what's all this? You want me to go back? Huh?"

Janet looked up at him, her long black lashes damp. "You all right, Rufus?" she whispered.

"Never better," said Rufus. He gave one of her pigtails a tug. "Man, I been missing those pigtails of yours! Wasn't a guy up there had pigtails I could pull."

Janet giggled through her sobs. As Mr. Travers came from the car, she drew back and wiped her eyes. She looked very neat and pretty, with her big eyes and her skin the color of dark honey. Rufus introduced Mr. Travers, and Janet murmured, "Hello."

"Where's Curtis?" asked Rufus.

"He's inside. Mama, too."

Then the door flew open and a small boy in T-shirt and jeans came down the walk. At top speed, Curtis collided with his brother. Rufus knuckled his hard little head with one hand, Curtis stepped back and looked at Mr. Travers, then at Rufus.

"Are—are you going to stay?" he asked.

"You bet. Isn't that so, Mr. Travers?"

"He sure is," said the officer.

Curtis dropped his glance to the walk. "Mama said for you all to come inside," he said. "She's not dressed for outside."

A shadow moved behind the screen door. Their mother was dressed, all right, Rufus knew. She didn't want the neighbors to see her with her jailbird son and his parole officer.

Sitting in the parlor with his family and the parole officer, Rufus sniffed the odor of antiquity of the house. It smelled about the way he would have expected the Chamber of Kings in a pyramid to smell. Scraps of rug were tossed about the floor, and the furniture was so sprung that, as he sat in an armchair, his hip pockets rested on the floor. The parlor was curtained from the hall by a screen of eucalyptus buds strung on thread.

Mr. Travers was explaining the conditions of Rufus's parole to Mrs. Henry. Rufus knew she wasn't listening, that she was listening to her own thoughts. She was a slender woman with dark-brown features; she wore a cool-looking green print dress. She had been cleaning house, and the corners of her red kerchief stuck up like rabbit's ears.

"Is everything clear, now?" Mr. Travers asked Rufus's mother.

"Yes, sir. Yes, sir," she said, wringing her hands together.

"Now, about school," said Mr. Travers. "It's too late in the semester for Rufus to start, so why don't we wait until next fall?"

Mrs. Henry nodded. "That be fine," she murmured.

"In the meantime, I have a job lined up for the boy."

"Yes, sir," Rufus's mother said.

It was quiet. Mr. Travers looked at her, seeming puzzled. "No problems you'd like to discuss, then?"

"Mr. Travers, sir," said Mrs. Henry, "things ain't going to be one bit different. He the same boy he was when he went away. An' so what am I going to do with this bad boy of mine the first time he get himself in trouble again?"

Curtis and Janet frowned at her. Rufus crossed his arms and smiled at the ceiling, humming to himself.

"Why don't we assume he's a good boy, Mrs. Henry?" Mr. Travers suggested. "His camp record was excellent. That's why he was released so soon."

Mrs. Henry sighed. Looking at her, Rufus wished she did not wear kerchiefs when she cleaned. It made her look like a slave, so that he was ashamed. He was ashamed, too, that she kept the blinds drawn in every house they lived in; that she kept papers stuffed in the mail slot to keep neighbors and welfare people from spying on her.

Yet through all these feelings ran a yearning for the time when he thought she really loved him, before he began getting in trouble. Long time ago, that was. Things changed; she grew inflexible and was always worried. He had had to learn to get along without her affection, the way fat people got along without sweets.

Mr. Travers closed Rufus's folder. Taking a card from his wallet, he wrote something on the back of it and handed it to Rufus.

Ace Tire & Retread. Mr. Wells, he had written.

"I've spoken to this man about you," he explained. "He'll give you a job, but it's up to you to keep it. See him tomorrow."

Rufus raised and dropped his shoulders and tucked the card in his pocket.

"Where will he sleep?" Mr. Travers asked Mrs. Henry.

"Upstairs," Mrs. Henry said. "Chil'ren, show Mr. Travers the room we fixed up."

The parole officer glanced at Rufus, but Rufus gave no indication of caring to see the room. Janet and Curtis skipped into the hallway, and Mr. Travers followed them.

As soon as they were gone, Rufus asked quickly, "You bring my scrapbook along?"

His mother nodded. "It's under your bed, just like you always kept it."

Rufus sank back into the chair. Then he said: "I'm sorry I messed up. Maybe I'll go back to school next fall."

"Ain't it fine about you having a job?" said his

mother. "Work's the best cure I knows for hell-raising. And you had that job last year in a tire-retread place, so you ought to do real good."

Rufus twisted his shoe sole on the worn carpet, frowning. "I'm still coughing up rubber dust, too. That's no job. It's a sentence."

"Maybe you can quit after a spell and get another job. They hires a lot of Negro boys in car washes and places like that."

"I've noticed that most guys that wash cars can't afford to drive one," Rufus said.

"So what you goin' to do?" his mother asked.

Rufus got up and took off his coat. "Go back to school, when it starts. I'm not going to be any career retreader. They made all these tests at camp. I did pretty good on the reading and figuring things out."

His mother smiled. "I hope you're going to figure things out better when you hit the sidewalk this time."

"I might decide to be a teacher or something. I get along good with little kids. And I read a lot of books up there. It's hard to know what to do."

For the first time that day he saw interest and affection in his mother's face.

"Well, if you want to go back to school, Rufus," she said, "I'll sure enough try to help you. Though I'm working myself sick paying the rent and taking care of your brother and sister. Wouldn't you have to go to college to be a teacher?" she asked.

"I guess. But maybe I could get a football scholarship. If I kept my grades up this time, I could stay on the team. And Coach Murphy said there wasn't anybody in California could catch me if my blockers sprung me loose. And that's the truth. I guess I come by it natural, huh?"

As if on signal, his mother got up, heavily. "I got

things to do, Rufus. I'm glad you're back. You be a good boy, now, because next time you might go to a real prison."

"Wait a minute," Rufus said. He crossed the room and peered into her face. He lowered his voice.

"One of the guys at camp said Ernie Brown was born and raised in Detroit. He said he heard him on TV once, and he doesn't have any Mississippi accent. So how could he have grown up in Leesburg?"

Mrs. Henry put her hands on her hips. "Now, what's he know about it? You going to believe him or your mother? You'll hear anything if you listen long enough."

"I'm listening now. Didn't you say you met him in Leesburg, Mississippi?"

"That's what I said. And I've got too much to do to talk about it now, so run along upstairs and see your room."

Rufus frowned after her for a moment, then strode from the room and hunted for the stairs.

At the far end of the dark vestibule was a narrow staircase that corkscrewed up through the ceiling. Rufus trotted up the stairs to the upper floor. There was a door at the rear, and an open door directly ahead of him. Inside the room he could see Mr. Travers standing with his hands on his hips, looking out the window at the freeway only a hundred feet behind the house. Cars and trucks flowed by in steady streams. Janet and Curtis were sitting on a narrow bed against one wall. Rufus moved into the doorway. He inspected the room with a feeling of pleasure. It was tiny and crooked, but snug; and it was all his. He didn't have to share it with fifty other guys and their radios and chatter.

Wedged up under the ridgepole of the house, it had a peaked ceiling like a tent. The ceiling sloped down to meet the half-height walls in such a way that one could hardly stand up straight except in the middle of the floor. There being no closet, his clothing hung on a cord stretched along the wall.

Mr. Travers said to Curtis, "And you have the other upstairs room, eh?"

"Uh-huh."

"I sleep downstairs with Mama," Janet said.

"Doesn't the girl usually get the private room?" the parole officer joked.

Janet looked down, embarrassed. "I get nightmares. So I rather sleep with Mama."

"May I see your room?" Mr. Travers asked Curtis. "If we got out, Rufus might be able to get into his own room."

As soon as they went out, Rufus stepped inside. He extended his arms, but his fingertips did not touch either wall. He smacked his fist against his palm, grinning, and walked to the window. Below his window was a small, fenced-in back yard with a chain-link fence at the rear marking the State's right-of-way. Though it was bare of anything but weeds and trash, and a half-dozen dying fruit trees, it somehow appealed to him. High board fences on the sides sustained an illusion of privacy.

Across the hall, Rufus could hear them talking in Curtis's room. He listened for a moment. Then he groped under his cot. He pulled out a big brown paper sack and sat on the bed with it. Carefully, he extricated a scrapbook as big as a metropolitan telephone directory.

On its cover was a picture of a Negro football player sitting on a bench, his helmet off and his brown face pensive. Above the picture he had crayoned the words:

BIG ERNIE BROWN
"ONE-MAN WRECKING CREW"

It was a sportswriter's phrase. Shots of Big Ernie crashing through the line, his face strained, his body full of grace and power. Closeups of him as a young college star.

It was almost eerie, Rufus thought, how much he looked like Ernie.

". . . Like football, Rufus?" said Mr. Travers's voice.

Rufus closed the book quickly. He rose and stared angrily. "Ever think of knocking, man?" he asked, his teeth bared.

The parole officer shrugged. "I'm sorry, Rufus. I wanted to say one last thing."

"I hear you, dad."

"Don't join the Moors. That's a condition of your parole. Look up Walter Gibson, if you want. I realize he was a friend of yours at camp. But don't join the gang he belongs to. Play it loose for a while. Okay?"

He offered his hand. Rufus looked at it; then, smiling tolerantly, accepted the handshake.

"Okay," he said.

FOUR

Rufus pulled off his State clothing and dressed in an old T-shirt and faded jeans. He was surprised to find the shirt much too tight for him through the shoulders. I really put on some beef up there, he realized. He decided the thing to do was to get a heavy job this summer, if he could find work at all. When a black boy found work, of course, it was going to be heavy: no problem there.

He flexed his shoulder muscles, taking pleasure in the strong and supple action of them. I got to eat right, too, he decided. For this body of his might make all the difference between carrying a lunch pail all his born days, and getting into some kind of work that paid a decent wage and was of some account in the world. Without education, a boy was dead; and the only way Rufus Henry would ever get through school was on scholarships.

He stepped out of his room, and Curtis and Janet were sitting on the floor with their backs against the balustrade of the stairs, waiting for him. They scrambled up.

"Haven't you kids got anything better to do than bird-dog your brother?" he asked.

"Huh-uh," Janet said.

"What you going to do?" Curtis asked.

"Stick around and you'll find out," Rufus said.

With them at his heels, he sniffed around the strange old house for a while, getting acquainted with it. There were five rooms, plus a cellar entered from outside. The wooden trim was paint-sick, a quarter-inch deep with layers of old paint. The plumbing was rusty, and the light switches were the old-fashioned kind that you twisted. Electric wiring squirmed up and down the walls like vines.

Rufus could not shake the feeling that at any minute a whistle would blow and someone would shout, "All right, you guys—make the dirt fly!" Though for the last month or so, he was one of the guys blowing the whistle. He would miss his work crew—ramrodding other kids around.

Maybe I ought to work for quarterback, he thought. But he was too valuable as a halfback, Coach Murphy always told him. Can't spare you, Rufus. You're my yardage-maker.

Suddenly he realized he was tired, nervously depleted by the big day that had begun before dawn at Pine Valley. He told Curtis and Janet:

"I'm going to lie down for a while. Go up and block the traffic on the freeway so it won't bother me."

They giggled and went out of his room. He heard them go into Curtis's room, so they would hear him as soon as he was stirring again. Got a feeling I'm going to see a lot of them for a while. Crazy kids. But he was pleased.

Stretched out on his cot, he listened sleepily to the diesels blatting by, the cars passing with a rising and falling *whoosh*. He leaned over and pulled out his Big Ernie book again.

As he turned the pages, Big Ernie smiled at him and glowered at him; snarled, laughed, and brooded.

The printed matter below one of his favorite pictures said:

> He is a huge man—six feet four, two hundred and forty pounds—whose body is tapered like a log-wedge. In action, he is fierce. At rest, he is reflective, sometimes sad. Because of his tremendous power, he has injured many players who got in his way. Ernie always reaches down to help a hurt player to his feet. "Excuse it, man," he says.

Rufus's eyes closed. Fatigue flowed over him like warm water. Pictures ran across his mind. He was hurrying over a dark playground late at night. Suddenly a dozen boys rose from the ground and surrounded him, swinging car aerials, brandishing knives. Rufus pulled his own switchblade and got his back to a small tree. A boy rushed him, and Rufus slashed him on the arm. Two more lunged, and he was cut across the hand. They moved in, silent and fierce. He was hurt, but still fighting desperately, when the gigantic shape of a man came trotting across the playground. The rays of a streetlight revealed his face.

Big Ernie Brown!

With a backhand blow, Ernie decked four of the boys, tire irons, knives, and all! Rufus jumped another and knocked him out with a blow to the chin. Soon all the attackers were down. Big Ernie went around helping them to their feet.

"Excuse it, man," he would say to each.

Rufus helped up the boy he had knocked down. "Excuse it, man," he said.

Now Rufus and Ernie were alone, as the boys ran off.

"I've got my Cadillac parked over yonder," Ernie said. "Care to go cruising? I'd like to talk to you about playing for the Corsairs. Liked the way you handled yourself in there."

"Why, sure, Ernie," Rufus said, dropping his knife in his pocket. "I'm agreeable."

A door hinge squeaked. Rufus raised his head, dazed with sleep. Curtis was peeking in at him.

"Mama wants us to pick mustard greens for supper," he said. "You want to see where we get 'em at?"

Rufus sat up, swung his feet to the floor, yawned, and scrubbed his face. "Sure," he muttered. "Long as you can't get any sleep around here anyway."

At the back of the lot, the kids had scooped out a little trench so that they could weasel beneath the chain-link fence into the State's right-of-way. Weeds grew everywhere. There were tangles of the little weed with spear-like seed pods that you could make scissors out of, and acres of taller weeds with yellow flowers. These were mustard plants; in the damp soil under the freeway they grew in lush beds.

"We just pick the inside leaves," Janet told Rufus. "The big ones are too tough to eat."

As they picked, Rufus saw something shining in the weeds. He picked up a metal disk and rubbed it with his sleeve. "What do you know? A practic'ly new Chrysler hubcap. Any of the neighbors drive an Imperial?"

"They throw junk over from the freeway after a wreck," Curtis explained.

"How about saving parts till we got enough for a car?" Rufus suggested.

Curtis laughed. But a minute or two later, his voice low and uneasy, he asked, "What you going to do now, Rufus?"

"About what?"

"Going to join a gang, aren't you?"

"Huh-uh. If I do, it'll violate my parole."

Curtis hesitated. "—I've been thinking about joining the Little Warriors," he whispered.

Rufus seized his arm. "You aren't joining anything!" he snapped.

Startled, Curtis pulled back. "Why not? The Projeck kids have chased me up and down every alley in the Flats. I hate this place. First time they catch me, they'll beat me. I got to join something for protection."

"You got a big brother. That's protection, isn't it? If any of those little punks bother you, it'll be between them and me, see?"

Curtis looked down. "The big kids'll be after you too, Rufus, soon as they see you on the street."

"Don't you worry about your big brother. I can take care of myself. But joining a gang means going to war with the police. Every time there's a crime committed, they'll roust you in off the street and question you. But the unconnected kids don't get bothered much."

"The gangs bother them, though."

Rufus shook his finger under Curtis's nose. "Jus' let me hear about you messing around with a gang, Curtis, and you got big trouble at home. You remember that."

It was ironic to be voicing the same arguments the law and the counselors had thrown at him for years. What Curtis said was true. But what he said was true, also: A boy with an older brother who had a reputation had a chance to stay neutral.

The family ate in the kitchen on a table with a short leg. Rufus stuffed newspaper under the leg so that the table wouldn't rock when he put his elbows on it.

"Good food, old lady," he said. "You got those cooks up there beat six ways from Sunday."

His mother smiled at him. "Yes, and I've only been cooking eighteen years," she said. "Curtis, did you get milk for breakfast like I told you?"

"No, ma'am. You never gave me enough money."

Rufus tilted his chair back and reached in his pocket. "I'll buy," he said. "The State gave me fifty dollars gate money."

"I was meaning to ask about that," his mother said.

"I'll split with you. Down the middle." From a copper money clip he had made at camp, he pulled a fold of bills. Counting off two tens and a five, he tossed them on the table.

"The kids and I will go down to the store and get the milk. You guys want some ice cream?"

Mrs. Henry raised her voice. "They ain't going two feet out of this house! Every night the Lord sends, there's some boy or girl beat up on the street."

"Not on the sidewalk, Mama!" Janet protested. "It's all right if you stay where it's light. *Please!*" she begged.

Mrs. Henry frowned at her. "Well—you can go if you want, but I ain't going to be left alone in this house. Curtis will have to stay here."

Curtis began to argue, but his mother picked up her table knife. "You want the handle of this here knife across your knuckles, young man?"

"We'll bring you something good, Curtis," Rufus promised.

Curtis left the table with tears in his eyes.

FIVE

Under the camphor trees, Rufus and Janet hurried toward Durango Street. Broken by tree roots, the sidewalk made hazardous walking. There was a softness to the night; down here it was already spring. Rufus saw people sitting on their porches. Occasionally he heard mellow laughter from the darkness. Once he smelled woodsmoke, and saw, in a vacant lot, a dozen people standing around a small barbecue fire burning in a hole. They looked like African tribesmen in a village. There was a delicious fragrance of spareribs on the air.

As they walked, he rolled his shoulders, getting the feel of freedom. It was as if a knapsack full of stones had dropped from his back. He shadow-boxed, dancing lightly on his toes as he fought an invisible opponent.

"Jab! Jab! *Cross!*" he muttered. "Jab! *Cross!*"

"You're out of your mind, Rufus." Janet laughed. Shyly she took his arm.

Rufus patted her hand. "You getting to be quite a girl, Janet. Soon be wearing your hair up, I expect."

"Not according to Mama. She'd like to put me in overalls so the boys wouldn't notice me."

Behind them a car approached with a deep burbling of exhaust pipes. It sounded like a powerful modified engine. He turned to watch it pass, but as it neared them it slowed. It was a cut-down sedan with its front end nearly scraping the asphalt. A car-club plaque was bolted to the bumper. It pulled in beside them, and stopped. Six or seven dark faces peered out at them.

Rufus whispered, "If they get out, run up on somebody's porch."

For ten seconds they stood under the silent scrutiny of the boys in the car. He heard a door latch click and set himself to push Janet toward the porch. Then a voice said, "It ain't him."

The engine revved up. A boy yelled, "Get off the street, punks!" As the car gunned away, the rear door opened and something was hurled at them. Rufus pivoted to shield his sister. A heavy object struck him between the shoulder blades. He gasped. There was a splintering crash as the object landed on the cement. Broken glass and torn paper covered the sidewalk. The boys had hurled a sack of bottles at them.

A screen door screeched. "What's going on here?" a man shouted.

Rufus reached around to rub his spine, his face somber. Letting himself be run off the street was no way to start off in a new neighborhood.

"Let's go home!" Janet whispered.

"No. They'd have jumped us on the first pass, if they meant to hurt us. But just in case—"

Among the fragments of glass, he found the neck of a bottle with a long curl of glass angling from it.

"Nobody's going to bother us now, sis," he said. "Come on."

They walked on toward the misty dome of light above Durango Street.

They had gone only a short distance when he heard a soft whirr of tires again. An automobile was creeping up on them with its engine idling and its lights out. Just as he turned, a blinding beam of light shot from the car. He knew then that it was a police car.

He kept his improvised knife hidden. The spotlight clicked off. It was a hand-spot held by one of the officers on the front seat.

"Know anything about that broken glass back there?" the officer called.

"No, sir," Rufus said.

"Where do you live?" the officer asked.

"Seven Fifty-nine Teagarden," Rufus said.

"Some boys threw them at us, Officer!" Janet piped up.

"Is that a fact. What boys?"

With a scowl, Rufus tried to tell her to keep quiet.

"Some boys in a car," she said.

"Did you see the license on the car?"

"No, but there was a sign on it that said, 'Gassers.'"

Rufus took her hand to hurry her on.

"Wait a minute, kids," the officer said. Rufus crossed his arms, and waited. "What's your name?" the officer asked him.

"Robert Jones."

"Is that your sister, Mr. Jones?"

"Uh-huh. Name's Alice."

"Well, Mr. Jones," said the officer, "did you see what color this car was?"

"It was blue gunmetal," Janet reported promptly. "There were seven or eight boys in it."

Rufus stared down the street, his eyes glazed with disgust and apprehension.

"How about that, Mr. Jones?" asked the officer, smiling.

"I couldn't see them, Officer. It was too dark."

"Did they say anything?" the officer asked Janet.

"Yes, sir. They told us to get off the street."

"Well, now, that's a coincidence. We were just looking for them to tell them the same thing. Those Gassers have no business being down here at all. Cathedral Heights is their beat. Which way were they headed?"

"Toward Durango," Janet reported.

The car began to move. "Thanks, kids," the policeman said.

The car swept away, a tiny cyclone of dry leaves whirling in its wake. Rufus shook Janet by the arm.

"For Pete's sake, girl! Don't you know you never tell a cop *anything?*"

"Why not, Rufus? We didn't do anything wrong."

"If they pick those cats up, they'll be looking for us next to identify them! How long you think we'll stay alive, if we do?"

Janet's eyes filled with tears. Disgusted, Rufus tossed the broken glass into some bushes. "You gotta get wise, girl. You want those Gassers clawing you up with beer openers? You want your brother beat' to death?"

Janet sobbed. Relenting, Rufus put his arm around her and gave her a reassuring squeeze. "I mean, you jus' don't talk to *anybody,* see? You don't tell 'em *anything,* not even if you see somebody beat' right before your eyes. 'Cause if you talk, it's you the wagon's carting off next time."

"We better go home, Rufus," Janet whimpered.

Rufus peered down the dark tunnel of the trees. A cold nervousness tightened around him.

"No, we better go on. If we go back without the milk, Mama'll know something happened. Like as not, she'll get all steamed up. Call my p.o."

They reached Durango Street. There was a dismal gaiety about this main trail through the Flats.

The soft radiance of neon was blurred by the fumes of automobiles and industrial plants. Men in shirt sleeves lounged around the doors of dingy taverns. Most of the stores and shops were closed. A block west, the small white taco stand Rufus had seen that afternoon was getting a big play. Small groups of boys and girls blocked the sidewalk.

As they went on, past dark shops where night lights burned like sickroom lamps, Rufus hid his tension behind a bouncing stride. They neared the taco stand.

"That's the Happy Spot," Janet said. "Mama won't let us go there."

"She's right this time."

Suddenly Janet clutched his arm. "Rufus!"

Rufus froze as he saw the car, too. It was the gun-metal sedan with the "Gassers" plaque on the bumper. Beside it, in the street, stood a half-dozen boys and a police officer. The officer wore a dark-blue uniform and a cap with a white crown. He had one of the boys backed against the side of the car.

Rufus pulled Janet into a doorway out of sight.

SIX

By twos and threes, the Happy Spot's patrons drifted off until there was no one left but the policeman, the boys he was questioning, and the second policeman who was searching under the front seat of the car with a flashlight.

The boys wore black jeans and a variety of coats and jackets; some sported bizarre high-crowned hats with half-inch brims. The boy the officer was questioning was a very light-skinned Negro. He wore a long corduroy car coat with a white muffler knotted about his throat. In the blue-white fluorescence of the taco stand, Rufus saw that his hair was a peculiar brindle color, almost orange. He wore it in a high, stiff brush.

Looking at the others, he saw that all of them had the same orange-red hair. "Gassed" was the name for it. You straightened your kinky hair with a paste made of mashed potatoes and lye. When you washed it off, you had straight hair. The next time it started to curl, you soaked it in gasoline to straighten it. Now it was straight again, but it was also red. Apparently the Gassers left their hair red as a trademark.

"We been right here for an hour," said the tall boy in the gray car coat.

"That the truth, Officer," said a smaller boy in a

mustard-colored T-shirt and enormous square sunglasses.

"You wouldn't know the truth if it was filed under T," the officer said disgustedly. "Why don't you punks stay where you belong?"

The leader shrugged. "We just cruising, Officer," he protested. "Any law against that?"

"If I find one, you're the first person I'll tell about it. I've seen you at the station, haven't I?"

"Maybe. They're alla time questioning me about something I didn't do."

"And you've been busted eight or ten times for things you did do. Isn't that so?"

The other boys chuckled, but kept their heads tipped down.

"Let's see your driver's license." The officer studied the cards in the boy's wallet. "Simon Jones, eh? I keep meeting people named Jones tonight. Wanted, by any chance?"

"No, *sir!*" Simon Jones said, solemnly. "I'm not one of them troublemakers."

The other officer came from the car. He had a handful of beer-can openers. "What are you carrying these around for?"

"Why, man, they—they just bottle openers!" said Simon Jones.

Janet tugged at Rufus's sleeve. "Let's go back!"

"No. They'd see us."

The officer dropped the can openers in his pocket. "All right, get out of here," he said.

The Gassers climbed back into the car. As Simon Jones started to slide under the wheel, he threw a quick glance up and down the sidewalk. Rufus felt his eyes lock on them in surprise. Then he got into the car and started the engine.

The gunmetal sedan charged up Durango. The police car headed into one of the housing project jungles that surrounded the little business district.

"Where's that grocery store?" Rufus asked quickly.

"Next block. Are we still going, Rufus?"

"Got to get off the street. Those cats will be looking for us. We'll have to kill some time in the store."

In the middle of the next block, beside an alley, was a small grocery store. Old-fashioned porcelain letters fixed to the inside of the window said: CHANG'S GROCERY.

"Mr. Chang's kind of funny," Janet whispered. "He doesn't like kids much. Don't touch anything."

Rufus sauntered inside. The store was so small that it looked like a playhouse. Along one wall were displayed fruits and vegetables, and here, working with meticulous care, a tall, stooped Chinese was arranging tomatoes in a pyramid. As the doorbell jingled, he wiped his hands on a long brown apron and peered at them. An old man with a long, lean head, he wore a black skullcap and round hornrimmed glasses. He was smoking a cigarette in an amber holder.

"Something?" he asked curtly.

Mr. Chang went behind the counter as though to watch the cash register. For a while Rufus and Janet moved up and down the aisles. Without warning, Mr. Chang appeared beside them, his face stern.

"What you looking for?" he demanded.

"Well, I'm trying to remember what we're s'posed to get. I'll think of it. Don't worry about us."

But Mr. Chang stuck right with them. By now, Rufus calculated, the Gassers had probably gone up to Cathedral Heights, made a U-turn, and were back running a block-by-block search for them. Alone, he might make it back; but he was stuck with Janet. They would have to stay off the street as long as possible.

"You buy what you want and get out. You no good!" Mr. Chang said abruptly.

Rufus looked him over. "What you talking about, old man? You don't even know me."

"I know you, all right. Know one boy, know all boys."

Rufus grinned at Janet. "Okay, Chief. Know where I can find a quart of milk?"

The old man hurried to the cooler and brought a carton of milk to the counter. Rufus followed him, stopping now and then to read the price on a can or carton. Shaking with anger, Mr. Chang put the milk in a paper sack and pushed it across the counter. Rufus frowned in thought, then pushed it back.

"Put in a couple of those chocolate bars, too," he said.

Breathing loudly through his nose, the Chinese dropped the candy in with the milk.

"How much we owe you?" asked Rufus.

"Thirty-four cents."

The doorbell jingled. Rufus kept his eyes from the door. He saw Janet's eyes widen. He turned and looked at a small Negro youth standing in the doorway. The boy wore a T-shirt and a green highboy hat. His long sideburns were red. He finished looking the place over, then turned abruptly and went out.

"I forgot something," Rufus said. "Our mama don't like milk in cartons. You got any bottles?"

Through the thick lenses of his glasses, the grocer's eyes regarded him with cold fire. Without a word, he carried the carton back to the refrigerator and returned with a bottle.

"Ten cents' deposit!"

Rufus paid the dime and picked up the sack. Outside, he peered up and down the street, seeing only normal street traffic. He gripped Janet's elbow. "Okay: head through the alley and cut home the back way!"

Janet was beginning to cry. "Aren't you coming with me?"

"I've got to slow those guys down."

"But you said they—they might—"

Grinning, Rufus bobbed his head like a fighter. "Those Gassers will just have to take their chances with me. Probably don't have any weapons, 'cause they just been rousted."

Down the block, exhaust pipes barked and tires squealed on streetcar tracks. Glancing back, Rufus saw a car making a U-turn. He gave Janet a spank.

"Head for home, now! Wait on the porch and we'll go in together, so Mama'll think nothing happened."

As she ran down the alley, Rufus leaned against a wall at the mouth of it. He saw her reach the far end and vanish into the darkness. But he lingered on the walk until he was sure the boys in the sedan had seen him; then he ran into the alley, looking for a doorway to hide in.

SEVEN

Fifty feet down the alley he found a shallow alcove with a couple of cartons of trash beside it. He stepped inside and found a metal-clad door with a padlock.

Putting his back to the door, he ripped open the paper bag and dropped the candy bars into his pocket. Then he let the milk bottle dangle from his hand.

The car entered the alley at high speed, its front bumper scraping the blacktop as it took the dip. The alley was brilliantly illuminated by its headlights. Rufus poked his head forward, then ducked back. Immediately the car stopped, the doors squealed open, and he heard the boys piling out. He waited until they were close. Then he stepped out.

The boys who were running toward the alcove stopped short and stared at him. There were seven of them. At the head of the pack was Simon Jones. Each youth carried a weapon scavenged from the street on a moment's notice—a chunk of cement, a piece of two-by-four, a beer-can opener.

"Oh, man! You done asked for it this time!" Simon panted. "You tol' the fuzz we threw them bottles, didn't you?"

"I didn't tell them anything," Rufus said. "I haven't got two words for any cop."

"You won't have," said the weird little monkey-like boy with the square sunglasses. "Not when we get done."

The boys fanned out in a semicircle around Rufus. His battle plan was made. It allowed little time for talk. Yet he wanted to try to salvage something of his plans: to try, if possible, to stay neutral.

"What's your name, man?" the gang leader asked. He moved forward, his coat falling open. A short length of iron pipe was shoved under his belt. In his hand he gripped a can opener, a steel claw to rake flesh to the bone.

"Rufus Henry. That's with a big R and a big H. Tell you what: tomorrow I'll meet you anyplace you say and we'll talk this over."

Simon glanced at the boy beside him. "Not a bad place to talk right here, ain't that so, Dukie?" he said.

"The best," said Dukie.

Rufus's muscles flickered as the boys began to tighten the noose on him. Simon was not yet close enough for him to make his move.

"Place is okay, but the time's not right," he said. "I can see you swing with the best of them, Simon. Reckon you can put the finger on me any time you want. So don't panic into throwing with somebody you don't know. You don't even know but what I pack a gun."

"I know you good," Simon said, moving closer and weaving his head from side to side like a coiled snake. "You're the cop lover. That's your name, boy: cop lover."

Suddenly a movement behind the boys caught Rufus's gaze. His eyes widened. He stared astonished at the far wall of the alley.

Against the bricks stood an enormous man, black from head to foot and at least seven feet tall! It was like a miracle. Big Ernie had come up through the pavement to save him. Standing there, he seemed to say:

Like the way you handle yourself in a scrap, Rufus—

Then one of the boys stirred, and the giant fled down the wall and vanished. With sickening deflation, Rufus realized that it was only the shadow of one of the Gassers, projected by the headlights.

Yet even the thought of Big Ernie bucked him up. In a level voice he said: "Stand still, now, alla you. Or somebody gonna get hurt."

Simon hefted the chunk of concrete he carried. "I reckon you know who's gonna get hurt," he said. He took another step forward.

Rufus tapped the milk bottle against the bricks. Glass jangled and milk splashed down the wall. The neck and half the bottle remained in his grasp. The glass tapered to a dagger-like point. The noise shocked the gang to a dead stop. Rufus took one step and was face to face with Simon Jones. He placed the sharp point against his stomach, letting him feel its edge through his T-shirt.

"Guess who's gonna get hurt, Simon," he said.

He saw the skin tighten over Simon's cheekbones. His lips trembled, but he stood fast—smart enough not to raise his weapon, too proud to start begging.

"What you want, man?" he gasped.

"I want the keys to your car."

Simon started to back off. "Sure, man. I'll get em."

"Don't run off, ol' yella man," Rufus warned. "Get 'em, Dukie. The rest of you cats lay down on your faces."

Dukie hesitated. "Well, get the keys!" Simon said, as Rufus stepped up the pressure against his belly.

"Turn off the headlights while you're at it," Rufus said.

The boy in the sunglasses squeezed between the car and the alley and reached into the front seat. The glare of the headlights dwindled and died. In the darkness, Rufus heard the boys begin to stir. He pressed the glass harder.

"Tell 'em to stay put," he said.

"You hear the man," Simon Jones said.

Dukie returned with a jingling set of keys and dropped them onto Rufus's palm.

"You gonna steal my car?" asked Simon.

"You going to the police if I do?"

"No. I can handle it."

Rufus looked over the half-dozen figures in the alley. "This all there is of the big bad Gassers?" he asked scornfully.

"There's sixteen of us," Simon said, "and I call in a couple other gangs when we're going to throw with somebody. Still want them keys?"

"Listen here, Simon," Rufus said earnestly. "This is the truth. I never talked to those police. They came by while the bottles were still practic'ly in the air. So I reckon they went looking for guys that didn't belong in the Flats."

Simon continued staring at him. None of the gang uttered a word. Under their silent scrutiny, Rufus waited. At last he tossed the keys on his palm. It was settled: there was no way to avoid going to war. Whether Simon believed him or not, street tradition forced him to refuse Rufus's explanation. Rufus had backed him down, and the only way to maintain control of a gang was to square with any newcomer who challenged you.

"Get back in the car," Rufus ordered. "I'll leave the keys at the other end of the alley."

He waited until the boys had climbed into the car. Then, trotting slow and easy like Big Ernie heading for the showers, he moved off down the alley.

Janet was weeping silently on the front steps when he returned home. She stared at him, amazed, as he came striding up the walk.

"Rufus? Aren't you hurt?"

"Girl," Rufus said, "have I got to kill a wild animal barehanded to convince you? Wipe your nose and let's go in."

Late that night, unable to sleep, Rufus padded downstairs and looked in the refrigerator. He made himself a peanut butter sandwich and drew a glass of water. He sat at the table and ate in solemn loneliness. He turned off the light and started back to bed. As he passed his mother's room, he heard a voice murmuring:

". . . You knows I done all I could for him. But he bound to get in trouble again. Young uns won't listen to nobody any more. Maybe if you talks to him, Lord—"

Rufus relaxed. She was only talking to Jesus. He had been afraid Janet had told her about the Gassers.

Shoot, man, he thought, maybe You *better* help! 'Cause I don't see how anybody else can. All the Mister Traverses and cops in this town can't keep a kid alive if he's not connected.

"Old lady?" he called softly. "You 'wake?"

A pause. Then: "What you doin' up, Rufus?" He could see her as he had so often, on her knees beside the bed.

"Want to talk to you about something."

"I don't want to talk to you. I got to be on that six-oh-three bus in the morning for work—"

"It's about Ernie Brown, Mama."

"Well, *what* about him?"

"I want to know whether you were really married to him."

A moment's silence. Then he heard his mother get to her feet; floorboards creaked as she crossed the floor. The door opened an inch. Inside the room it was dark. His mother whispered:

"You go on back to bed, Rufus! I done talked about that man all I mean to! I was just a little bitty girl sixteen years old when we was married, and it was all over in a few months. I'm sorry I ever told you. You go around telling your social workers and gang friends, and it gonna make us both look silly. 'Cause who's going to believe us?"

"And then you got married again right away?" Rufus asked, a note of pleading in his voice.

But his mother closed the door. After a moment Rufus went back upstairs.

EIGHT

At six-thirty in the morning, the rumble of traffic jarred Rufus awake. He gazed up at the peaked ceiling of his tiny room. The timid light of dawn stained everything pink; a warm breath of air puffed against the ragged curtain, promising a fine day. As he lay there, comfort and pleasure seeped through him. Up at Pine Valley there was still ice in the ruts every morning; down here it was spring.

Then he remembered the clash with Simon Jones. His spirits sank.

In a couple of hours the Gassers would be out ransacking the Flats for him. Not in a pack that the police might notice, but like sharks, silent and deadly. Just a few boys drifting along, sober-faced, glancing into stores and alleys; or a boy idling on a street-corner, watching the traffic and behaving himself.

But a single, whistled note—a telephone call from a cigar store—and the sharks would form into a pack. And Rufus Henry would have his back to the wall in another alley—their alley, this time.

He sighed and sat on the edge of the bed. He wondered if he could find Baby Gibson in time.

Baby had said that his gang, the Moors, generally

hung out at the Happy Spot. A real fighting gang, Baby vowed. That's what I need, Rufus thought glumly. You can't fight 'em alone. There was comfort in thinking about Baby, who was well over six feet tall, deep-chested and powerful. He had taken up weight-lifting at camp, and Rufus had seen him prone-press more than his own weight: two hundred and twenty-five pounds.

But most of Baby's power was in his muscles, for he had had a brain injury and was incapable of schoolwork. And sometimes his temper took charge of him, and then it was like a bull elephant running amuck. Baby had been doing time at Pine Valley for hitting a man during one of these fits. The man had beaten a friend of Baby's whom he'd caught stealing a sandwich from his store; but it did not change the fact that Baby broke his jaw.

It was not the first time he had been in trouble, but it was his first visit to a Youth Authority facility. People were getting the idea he was dangerous.

At camp, he and Rufus were good friends. Each offered something the other seemed to need. When Rufus saw one of Baby's destructive moods building, he was the one who got him busy lifting weights or telling about some of the Moors' big rumbles until the feeling was off him.

The old house echoed with silence. When he went downstairs, Rufus found that everyone had left: his mother for work, Curtis and Janet for school. He poured cereal in a bowl and looked for milk in the refrigerator. But there was no milk. He had forgotten. . . . He threw out the cereal, tracked down a warm coke in the cupboard, and dropped a piece of bread into the toaster. He drank the coke and ate some toast.

He remembered, then, that he had a date with Ace

Tire & Retread today. He could smell the cooking rubber and dirty steam, and hear the hiss and clank of recapping machinery. He had hated the other tire shop; yet there was no getting around it: he must, at least, show up and ask for work.

Through the ragged curtains, he studied the street. A few small children were playing on the walks. In the driveway next door, a man was hammering on a dilapidated dump truck. Everything looked peaceful. But no matter how peaceful things might appear, the street was still the place where things happened. *And if anything happens before I lash up with the Moors,* he thought, *I won't be around to find them when the Gassers get through with me.*

Behind the house across the street he glimpsed an alley. The sight of it made him feel better. He always felt safer in an alley. There were always escape hatches in an alley, for a kid who could crawl, climb, or run. Before leaving, he looked over his mother's butcher knives. But after a moment he shoved the knifedrawer closed. He didn't dare be caught with a weapon on him.

He crossed the street and headed toward Durango Street. As soon as he saw a clear space between two houses, he hurried back to the alley. Peering east, he could see that it ended at Durango, an unpaved, disheveled roadway lined with fences hammered together out of old billboards, crates, and flattened-out tin cans.

When he reached Durango, he stood a full minute studying the traffic. He waited. Up the street he saw a bus lumbering along. When it reached his block, he trotted to the corner and boarded it. The bus carried him to the river and across the railroad yards to a grimy industrial district.

The tire shop was behind a truckers' service station. It was a low-ceilinged place full of molds like silver doughnuts laid in nests of pipes. Tires were cooking inside these molds. At various machines, tire casings were being stripped or worn-out treads examined for flaws, and roughed so that their raw surfaces would bond with the recap. Most of the employees were young men, seemingly tense and in a hurry, their faces grimy with dirt and sweat.

At the far end of the building Rufus saw an office. He entered it. A woman was operating an adding machine, while a big crew-cut man with rolled sleeves talked on the telephone. The man hung up and stared at Rufus.

"What's on your mind, boy?" he asked.

Rufus rolled a slow glance around the office. *Boy:* he wrinkled his nose. If you were black, you were "boy" until you were eighty. Then you were "uncle."

"Well?" the man said.

"I'm looking for Mr. Wells."

"That's me."

"Well, I'm Rufus Henry."

"So?"

"You're holding a job for me, they said."

"Oh. You're the jailbird," Mr. Wells said. Then he grinned. "Whoops. I wasn't supposed to say that. Come on—"

Rufus followed him, his eyes narrow with displeasure, his face impassive. The man halted beside a grinder fitted with a stiff wire brush. There was a mountain of dirty tire casings heaped beside it.

"Travers says you worked in a recapping shop once."

"Yes."

"Did you ever rough casings?"

"Uh-huh."

"These have been stripped. They need to be taken

down to the fabric, but not into it. You follow me, boy?"

"I dig."

Mr. Wells slapped him on the back. "I've got all the tools counted," he said, "so we ought to get along fine. You want to try it?"

He was grinning, and other workmen heard him and watched Rufus. Rufus picked up one of the carcasses and examined it.

"Okay," he said.

Rufus switched on the buffer and began burring the slick black rubber. His eyes were bitter. He glanced up and looked at the office. Mr. Wells was working at his desk. *Boy. Jailbird. Here's one for you,* Rufus thought. He held the tire against the wire brush until the fabric came through the rubber. Then he tossed it into the finish-pile.

Mr. Wells returned as he was working on the second casing. Rufus clenched his teeth, waiting. . . . "Pretty good," the man said. Then he saw the dollar-sized flaw.

"For Pete's sake, Henry! I thought you said you knew how to do it?"

"It'll take me a while to get back in practice," Rufus muttered.

"While you're getting back in practice, it's going to cost you three dollars per mistake. That's what a casing's worth. In two hours you'll be back to zero again."

He hurled the carcass aside, gave Rufus a stare, and walked away.

Rufus worked calmly and steadily. He finished two tires and laid them aside. Then he did four more, grinding a hole completely through the fabric of each. He kept the good casings on top, in case the manager came back.

Presently Mr. Wells did so.

"That's more like it," he said, examing the casing on the top. A horn honked and he walked out to take care of a customer.

Rufus ground two more tires, bringing daylight through each before he set it aside. Then he placed the good ones on the top of the pile and went to the office.

"Okay if I get a cup of coffee?" he asked Mr. Wells.

"How many have you done?"

"Seven."

"Take five minutes," the manager said.

Rufus crossed the street and started walking. In his mind the episode was over. He would never go back, and Mr. Travers would think twice before finding him another job. When he was ready—when he had found the Moors and made his connections—he would look for other work until school started. But it would not be in a place where they called you "boy" and "jailbird."

The Flats were quiet in midafternoon when he dropped off the bus. As it roared away in a dragon's-breath of fumes, he studied Durango. Across the street, the Happy Spot appeared deserted except for the middle-aged Mexican cook inside the aluminum and glass shack that comprised the kitchen. He crossed over, combing rubber dust out of his hair, and went up to the window.

"Cup of coffee," he said.

Somewhere he heard the swingy, nasal tones of a harmonica. While the cook drew his coffee, he glanced around. Between the kitchen shack and a brick building next door was a space about ten feet wide where the four redwood picnic tables were placed. Overhead was a sagging shelter of laths festooned with plastic leaves and roses. Only the rear table was occupied. He saw that this was where the music was coming from.

Five Negro boys sat at the table; one of them was playing a harmonica. Beside this boy sat a powerful youth with arms like thighs. It was Baby Gibson. Baby was bobbing his head in time to the music. The other boys were talking in the negligent manner of bored and restless youngsters.

Rufus carried his coffee back. Baby still had not seen him. With his mellow brown skin, he made Rufus think of one of those chocolate Easter bunnies that look solid but never are. But Baby was solid. Rufus had boxed with him at camp and been battered to his knees in two rounds. Anyone could hit him, but no one could hurt him.

At Baby's right sat a somber youth with long black hair straightened and plastered down. He wore a tuft of chin whiskers. The sleeves of his black shirt were rolled and a small Tyrolean hat was cocked over one eye. He straightened perceptibly as Rufus approached. Baby looked up, then, and suddenly came to his feet.

"Hey, looka here!" he exclaimed. He came to meet Rufus.

"How you been?" Rufus asked, grinning.

Baby punched his shoulder. Though it was only a playful blow, the shock spilled half of Rufus's coffee.

"Good! When you get back, man?" he asked.

"Yesterday."

"Whereat you living?"

"Teagarden Street. My old lady's got a house there. Kitchen overlaps the fast lane of the freeway."

Baby laid his arm across Rufus's shoulders. "Come

on back and meet some guys," he said.

The youth with the chin beard watched Rufus every foot of the way. Up close, his eyes were narrow and bloodshot.

"This is that guy I was telling you about," Baby told him proudly. "Name's Rufus Henry. This here's Richard Motley, Rufus," he said, indicating the boy with the chin beard. "We calls him Bantu. He's president of the Moors."

Rufus smiled into Bantu's eyes and offered his hand. "Glad to know you, Bantu," he said.

The gang leader was stripping a cigarette butt, tearing the paper and shaking tobacco onto the table as he studied Rufus. He made no move to shake hands.

"Okay if he sets down?" Baby asked Bantu.

Bantu made a careless gesture of assent. Rufus silently took a seat across from him between the other two boys. Bantu struck a match, set fire to a corner of the cigarette paper, and watched it burn.

Baby slapped the back of the boy at Rufus's right. "This here's Whitey," he said. Rufus turned his head to look at Whitey, who was about his own age, neat, slender, and good-looking, with fine features as blue-black as a pistol. The boy wore dark glasses.

"Glad to know you," Rufus said.

"Hi," Whitey said, deadpan.

"An' that's Ever't," said Baby.

Everett, at Rufus's left, was a thin boy with a small, skinned-looking head. He did not look as though he would be very fierce in a fight, but with his lean build he could probably do something almost as useful: run for help. He muttered something and looked away.

"This here's Willie Clanton," Baby said, placing his hand on the shoulder of the boy with the harmonica.

Willie had a large mouth and sleepy eyes. There was a slight jeer in the grin he gave Rufus. Rufus said, "Hello," and Willie replied in a bone-lazy voice, "Ha you, man?" and tossed the harmonica on his palm. There was a clicking sound, and from one end of the instrument popped a long, thin knife blade. Willie bent over the table top and began touching up a word someone had carved into the redwood. He seemed to have forgotten Rufus.

"How's everything at camp?" asked Baby.

" 'Bout the same," said Rufus. He felt cool with relief. *Safe on first!* he thought. "They're still handing it out that if you learn a good trade like cobbling, you're practically certain to be President."

"That goes whether you black or white?" asked Bantu, watching the paper burn.

Rufus chuckled. "I reckon. Hate to think all that time I spent learning to mend shoes was wasted."

Baby laughed. The warm sparks in his eyes told Rufus how glad he was that he was here. But Richard Motley, called Bantu, had not decided yet to be glad, and since the others took their cue from him, the atmosphere was charged with invisible particles of hostility.

"You spent your gate money yet?" Baby asked.

"Some of it."

"We'll throw us a party with the rest," Baby said.

"Okay."

"Who's your p.o.?" asked Bantu.

"Mr. Travers."

"Travers is a bum," said Bantu. "First traffic ticket you get, he'll let 'em send you back to camp. Wait and see."

"Nothing new about that," Rufus commented. "I

hear a parole officer is just a cop with his brains knocked out."

The boys laughed. But Bantu dropped the glowing cigarette paper on the table and blew it across the scarred redwood into Rufus's lap. Staring at Bantu, Rufus rubbed the sparks out against his jeans. The laughter dwindled.

This guy and me, thought Rufus, *aren't about to hit it off. Not in ten years.*

Bantu said slowly: "Hear you tangled with Simon Jones last night."

"Uh-huh."

"So now you want to join the Moors for protection. That the way it goes?"

"Maybe," Rufus said, uncomfortably. "Thought we could talk about it."

Bantu cocked his head inquiringly. "I don't dig that 'maybe,' boy. Either you in trouble or you ain't. Which is it?"

"Well, I got a little trouble, but—"

Bantu raised his voice. "Make up your mind. You want in or not?"

Rufus bit his lip, chagrined that the president had to use his need to humiliate him. He rubbed his hands on his thighs. "Yeah. I want in," he muttered.

"Thass too bad," said Bantu. "Because I hold the membership to guys that lives on the Big Lawn."

Rufus looked up. "Where's that?"

"The Projecks," Baby told him. "There's all this lawn around the buildings, you know. Man, I don't see what difference it makes," he said to Bantu. "Idell don't live on the Big Lawn."

"He live right across the street though, daddy," retorted Bantu.

The boys were silent. Rufus's mouth drooped. He

watched the small-headed boy named Willie finish carving in the table top:

MOORS IS BOSS

"Boss" meant tops; the best there was. Rufus had begun to doubt it.

Baby, sitting beside the gang leader, pulled away to scowl at him. Rufus feared that he was steaming up; and this was no time for a fight. Not if Rufus Henry was going to talk his way into the Moors, and there was nowhere else to go, short of the morgue.

"Listen here," Baby said warningly. "Rufus is a buddy of mine. You can't jes'—"

"I can't, huh?" Bantu said, glancing at him.

Baby stood up. "Hey," Rufus said. Baby looked at him, his eyes narrow and sullen; Rufus shook his head. "Hold everything," he said. Baby turned to stare challengingly at Bantu. Bantu seemed unaware that he was in any danger. Either he was mighty slow to catch on or he was sure of being able to handle the giant. Then Rufus saw that Willie Clanton had stopped carving and left the harmonica-knife stuck in the table in front of Bantu.

Bantu began talking. Baby slowly sat down.

"You askin' a lot, man," Bantu said to Rufus. "There's been a Moors gang in the Flats for thirty years. Guys gets too old and drops out, or go to jail, or they gets burned in a fight. I been president for nearly two years. You don't just say, 'Open the door, I'm comin' in,' 'cause you need protection. That where you show you're just a field nigger. We takes guys because they got something we want, not because they're in a jam with some gang from Cathedral Heights."

Rufus nodded in slow agreement. "I know. But I'm in a hurry to get connected," he said. "Those guys were going to slice me up and hang me on a line last night. You ever throw with them?" he asked.

"Not lately. They leaves us pretty much alone, unless we're up in their beat.

"How come they were down here last night, then?" asked Rufus. "Isn't this *your* beat?"

Bantu raised a suspicious glance to his face. But Rufus maintained a look of innocence.

"You better believe it is, man. But the heat's on me right now for droppin' pills. They know I got to stay clean for a while."

Rufus scratched his head. "You a user?" he asked.

"No. I don't use. But everybody drops pills. When you drops a couple of yellajackets and washes them down with a can of beer—you clear out of this world, Henry!"

The other boys laughed and nodded, except Baby, who sat there with a troubled and resentful face.

"Looks to me like you got to stop Jones pretty soon," Rufus commented. "I mean, those cats were all over the Flats last night."

"When I ready to move, Henry, you'll hear about it. I been busted for aggravated assault, car clout, and more raps than you ever see on one sheet of paper. Last year they queried me about a cop killin'. But I could prove I was on the Big Lawn. What makes you think I'd take a nothin' cat like you, anyway?" he asked, scornfully.

Rufus shrugged. "Just thought I'd ask." He stood up. There was no point in begging. It was up to Bantu, now; he could write him a letter about it, if that was how he operated.

Bantu grinned, showing long yellow teeth. "Aw, set down," he said. "I was just testing you. But I'll have to take a vote of all the guys before I can say for sure."

Rufus sat down. Baby, for the first time, relaxed and smiled.

"When's that going to be?" Rufus asked Bantu.

"Make a phone call, man," Bantu told Whitey. "Tell Idell we'll meet 'em at the playground at eight o'clock tonight. Got it?"

The trim black boy at Rufus's right nodded. "I got it. But I ain't got a dime," he said.

"Give him a dime," Bantu told Rufus.

Rufus worked a dime from his pocket. Whitey moved off toward the phone booth. Bantu said to Rufus, "You better get off the street. We'll pick you up here at eight o'clock."

NINE

At dinner, Rufus's mother asked: "How you like your new home by now, boy?" She seemed tired from her long day's work of house cleaning, but she was more relaxed than when he had first arrived.

"Fine," Rufus mumbled, holding a sparerib like a corncob.

"You try to find work today?"

"Uh-huh."

Mrs. Henry lowered her fork. "Find anything?"

"Sure. Already got a job," Rufus said.

They stared at him. Rufus inserted a final rib lengthwise in his mouth like a sword swallower, husking the meat off as he withdrew it.

"What kind of work you find, Rufus?"

"I'm a collector for the Phone Company. People forget to fish their dimes out of the slot when the call doesn't go through. Then a collector like me comes along."

He grinned at Curtis and Janet and headed out. "I'll see you. Got to punch that clock."

"Rufus!"

He was out the front door while his mother's call still reverberated in the house. Standing on the sidewalk, he sniffed the night. In the warm city air there was an acridness of smog and burning trash. Something else was in the air, too, that made his flesh crawl, something more intangible than smoke, a vibration of danger and excitement that caused certain feelers in his mind to quiver. He was not sure what it meant, but it probably signified that the Gassers had been around, and because word was out that they were on the prowl, other kids were staying off the street. Things looked suspiciously quiet.

He cut across to the alley. All the way to the Chinaman's, the only life he saw was a dog and a couple of cats. From the mouth of the alley, he looked up and down Durango, then swung down to the corner and studied the Happy Spot.

Five of the Moors were gathered beside an old green Pontiac parked before the taco stand. The boy called Whitey was sitting on a front fender that had been repainted, while Bantu leaned against a door, smoking a cigarette. As Rufus walked up, Bantu dropped his cigarette on the sidewalk.

Rufus grinned at the Moors. "What's the word?" he asked.

All but the leader spoke to him, but they seemed embarrassed. Even Baby had little to say, beyond introducing a boy Rufus had not met that afternoon.

"This is Marshall Smith," he said.

Marshall was about twenty, clean and handsome and with dimples that showed when he grinned. He wore a long yellow coat and black pants. As he gazed at Rufus, he tossed the biggest bunch of keys Rufus had ever seen. They must have weighed five pounds. The likelihood was that Marshall did not own a lock at all, but, swung on their long chain, the keys might serve as a weapon.

It was silent, now, as Bantu stared at Rufus. He smelled of liquor, and wore dark glasses to camouflage his bloodshot eyes. *Man, my little brother knows better than to wear sunglasses at night,* Rufus thought scornfully. *Just as well hang a sign around your neck for all the cops to read:* DRUNK AS A SKUNK.

Bantu spoke sullenly. "Eight o'clock don't mean eight-fifteen."

"Had to shake my old lady. This the car we're going in?"

Whitey nodded. "It's my mother's."

"Nice two-tone job. Green, with a red fender."

Whitey chuckled, but Bantu interrupted sharply. "Less cut the yakkin' and take off."

Rufus got in back with Baby, Everett, and Marshall. Baby did not reply when Rufus asked him how things were. Marshall kept jingling his handful of keys. Bantu and Whitey got in the front seat, and Whitey kicked the engine to life. It ran so unevenly that the whole car throbbed. The rear spring was broken, so that the automobile tilted to one side like a foundered ship. They rolled down a curving street through one of the housing projects. Acres of worn-out grass engulfed the buildings. A few blocks farther on, the project ended at a chain-link fence enclosing a large unlighted playground. A parallel street bounded the playground on the south. Rufus made out the silhouettes of play equipment in its vast blackness.

The fence ended at the next corner. Here a shabby old mission-style building stood, its windows dark. An automobile was parked near the corner. Whitey parked behind it and switched off the engine. Rufus expected to see the other members of the gang, but no one was in sight.

"Where is everybody?" he asked.

"We meets out in the playground," Bantu muttered.

They got out, looked around, and one by one, using the rough trunk of a palm tree as a ladder, dropped over the fence into the playground. Scorning the tree, Rufus ran up the chain-link fence and dropped inside.

The boys were trotting out into the jungle of courts beyond the playground building. But when he started to follow, Baby's hand closed on his arm.

"Us last," he said.

"What's going on?" Rufus asked, low.

Baby kept peering into the darkness as if waiting for a signal. "Well, uh, we got to take this vote," he said.

"That all?" Rufus asked, suspiciously.

Out in the darkness, a match flared briefly. Baby said "Okay," and jogged into the playground. Rufus stayed at his side. He felt as though he were floating in space as they traveled. There were no lights anywhere to tie him down to earth. It was black above, below, and at all sides. They passed a basketball backstop, and Baby slowed to a walk. Now Rufus could see the triangular uprights of a handball court. The backwall was high, with slanting sides. At the base line of the court, Baby halted.

"Stand here," he said. He walked into the deeper

shadows of the high wooden wall forming the back-wall of the court.

The silence seemed to thicken. After a time Rufus could see a dozen or more boys squatting against the wall. Then a match flared with a sizzling brilliance. He saw Bantu's long face and straggly chin beard. Bantu cupped the match in his hand to fashion a sort of lamp. Suddenly all of the Moors struck matches: he was surprised by the volume of light blazing up at him like footlights.

"This is the guy that wants to join the gang," said Bantu, after a moment. "Whatchyou guys think about him?"

"Who told you about the Moors?" a voice challenged.

"Baby Gibson," Rufus said. "We were buddies at Pine Valley."

"What was you doing time for?"

"Grand theft auto."

"That all?" asked another voice.

"Uh-huh. I've been busted for other things, other times."

"What kind of things?"

"Gang fighting and stuff. A.D.W."

"Assault with a deadly weapon? My, my! Unprovoked water pistol attackt?"

"Knife," Rufus said.

"Oh, you a blade man?"

"Not any more. I don't carry weapons if I can help it. I can usually find something if I need a weapon."

As the questioning continued, Rufus began to discern the faces of his inquisitors. Some of the Moors wore brimless highboy hats. None wore jackets—jackets cost money, and these were a poor looking bunch of boys.

"How much money you got?" asked Bantu.

"About twenty dollars."

Bantu slouched forward, his hand extended. Rufus, with a sigh, pulled his money clip from his pocket and surrendered it. Bantu pocketed the money.

"Now, if we takes you in," he said, "you got to do something to prove ·you're the kind we wants. You got to get yourself a can of red spray paint and go up to Cathedral Division police station. And you writes on the wall by the front door, 'Moors is boss.' You still with us, Henry?"

Rufus swallowed. "I'm still with you."

"Put out the matches," ordered Bantu. The sudden darkness took Rufus's breath. "Anybody that don't want him in, light a match."

A match was scratched. Another popped, then a third. After that there were no more.

"You in, man," Bantu said. "You a Moor." He offered his hand, smiling sleepily.

Rufus felt weak with relief. But as he accepted the leader's grip, the strong thin fingers closed on his like a trap. Bantu yanked him off-balance. At the same instant, his other hand came in from the side. Something heavy and jagged smashed against Rufus's cheekbone. There was a roaring in his ears; a hot pain at the point of impact melted like wax down the side of his face. He reached out for support, but there was nothing to grasp, and he fell to his knees. Feet shuffled quickly over the blacktop, as Bantu chuckled:

"Forgot to tell you, Henry. You gets beat' into this gang, and you gets beat' out."

Rufus staggered to his feet and looked up. He looked for Baby, hurt and puzzled. Why hadn't his friend warned him? Yet he realized that Baby was a Moor first, a friend second. For his own good, he had to live by the Moors' code.

Bantu was circling for a swing at Rufus's head. In his palm he gripped an old automobile crown gear. Another boy was moving in from the left, a short length of black hose in his hand. Marshall Smith was swinging his heavy knout of keys on its long brass chain, waiting for a clear shot. Alone against the forewall of the court, Baby waited with his arms crossed.

As Bantu lunged, Rufus ducked under his swing. The gang leader was slow and clumsy. Rufus stabbed his fist into Bantu's face, and a pleasant shock ran up his arm. Bantu dropped the gear. Rufus laughed. "You slow, man!" He hit him twice more before the boy with the hose was on him.

He caught this boy's wrist and forced his arm high, completing the motion with an elbow in the face. The kids yelled angrily as the Moor staggered back, as though the blow had been an unfair one. Another Moor tackled him around the waist. Three more boys piled on and they all went down. They were snarling and yelling and swinging wildly. Rufus fought with the silent bitterness of a cornered animal. He wriggled out from under the mass and got up. The way was open to run, now, if he wanted to. But if he ran he was out. If he stayed, he would either be in or so badly beaten it didn't matter whether he was in or out.

He set his jaw and waited.

Baby was still standing apart from the action. He could not prevent it, but he did not have to take part in it. Suddenly Marshall hurled his keys, the chain flashing around like the tail of a comet. Rufus ducked, but the chain lashed tightly about his neck. He tried to unwrap it, choking, as three other Moors darted in. He staggered to the sideline and crawled up the buttress-like sidewall. He was seven feet above them, and clawing frantically at the chain. Just as one of the youths started after him, he pulled the chain free.

Rufus hurled the keys in his face. Another boy climbed toward him with a car aerial raised like a whip. Rufus jumped onto the pack of boys gathered below him. They went to the ground in a threshing tangle.

He was the first up, throwing punches as the others scrambled to their feet. One boy stayed down. The boy called Whitey maneuvered Rufus into a corner and tried to box him. He had a pretty good jab, but when he skinned Rufus's brow and attempted to follow with a cross, Rufus stepped in quickly and smacked one into his nose. With a groan, Whitey covered his face and turned away.

Rufus whirled to face another of his attackers.

Without warning, the night exploded like a hand grenade.

A voice larger than any human voice—a deep, gut-shaking voice terrifyingly magnified and distorted—seemed to blast down at them from the sky.

"All right, you punks!" the voice roared. *"Break it up!"*

The boys crouched. In the silence, Rufus heard the purring of an automobile engine. A spotlight drenched the court with shadowless brilliance. Headlights snapped on; then a revolving red light atop a police car flashed.

Again the police bullhorn rattled the old wooden structures. "Face the wall and raise your hands."

Bantu yelled: *"Take off!"* He jumped a sidewall and went dodging through the maze of courts.

Across the playground the lights of another police car blazed. Wheels spun as it raced along the chain-link fence to block Bantu's escape. He swerved and sprinted across the dark earth toward the far side of the playground. The prowl car followed with its siren shrieking.

Rufus sank to his knees, numb with despair. He was bloody and pummeled, but scarcely aware of pain. His agony was too deep for even pain to reach. *They might as well have thrown away the key the first time they jailed me,* he thought.

You were licked if you got in trouble, licked if you tried to stay out. How else could you play their game?

Baby leaned over and helped him to his feet. "Sorry, Rufe," he whispered. "Tried to talk him out of it."

Rufus swayed there, watching the police line the boys up facing the wall. "What do we do now?" Baby asked.

Rufus shook off his hand. "Do like the man said. Face the wall. Maybe that's where the answers are. . . ."

At twelve-fifteen that night, Parole Officer Ed Travers left Cathedral Heights police station and walked to an all-night café to make a telephone call. Most of the Moors had been released to their parents or guardians. Bantu had been held for possession of drugs. Travers had preferred not to make this particular call from the station. Policemen were inclined to consider most p.o.'s fuzzy-headed do-gooders anyway, and Travers feared that in this case they might be right.

For he was about to waste a dime on Rufus Henry. And Rufus was not worth a dime.

He had been warned not to join a gang; but no sooner had he been turned loose than he had done so. What went on in the heads of kids like Rufus? Travers wondered. He did not pretend to understand such youngsters. They were totally different from the loners he usually dealt with, for the Rufus Henrys stuck together like suvivors of an ambush. They felt menaced unless they were with others of their own cult of violence.

In the telephone booth, he studied a business card. *Group Service Council* read the legend above a set of telephone numbers. The agency specialized in breaking up gangs. He had met the director several months ago, and was intrigued, though troubled, by what the man told him about his work. He shuddered at the picture of a bright-eyed young social worker joining the Moors at one of their hangouts and explaining, over a cup of coffee, how he was going to break up their club.

Nevertheless, it was a chance—Rufus's last. He dropped a dime in the telephone and began to dial.

TEN

At ten-thirty the next morning, a tall Negro in a dark business suit entered Cathedral Heights police station. Cathedral was the oldest police station in the city, a grimy fortress of dun-colored brick. He climbed the stairs to the second floor and opened the door marked *Juvenile Division*. He was hatless, and carried a folder in one hand. Lithe and long-legged, he had the appearance of an athlete dressed for the street.

A plain-clothes officer at a desk near the door glanced up. The plaque on his desk read *Sgt. Starkey. Commander.*

"Excuse me, Sergeant," said the visitor. "I'm Alex Robbins—with Group Service Council."

The sergeant leaned back, a burly man with a freckled face. "Come on in. Your boss said you'd be over. I hear you're going to put the Department on a paying basis," he added, grinning.

The social worker smiled. "Well, we hope to save you a little money on the Moors group, at least. Are you holding any of them?"

"Only Richard Motley. He's in Juvenile Hall on narcotics charges."

"Do you have their records handy?"

"Handy! I keep most of them right on my desk," Starkey replied. "It saves me from having to get out of my chair every time the telephone rings."

He collected a batch of thirteen folders and handed them to the visitor. Then he led him to a cell-like office. "You can read them in here."

The office was hot and stuffy with stale tobacco smoke. The social worker hung his coat over the back of a chair.

"Pardon the curiosity," the sergeant said, "but what do you hope to accomplish with these kids?"

"Break up their gang," said the Negro, smiling.

Starkey snorted. "Lots of luck, brother! The police have been breaking up the Moors gang for thirty years. And they snap back together like drops of mercury. Why not tackle something easy? Eliminate all the Smiths from Coast City. How did you poor souls happen to pick the Moors?" he asked, curiously.

Alex Robbins smiled, but his large, mild eyes were very serious. Under the naked light globe his skin had a brown metallic sheen.

"It's a long story," he said. "Parole officers and school principals have been calling us about them for a year. We've already made some inquiries into their backgrounds. Last night we had another call. The director decided to move in on them before it was too late."

"Do you want my opinion?" the sergeant said. "It's been too late for years. Crime is the way these guys get their jollies. I'll give you odds most of them are doing hard time before Christmas."

"Maybe," the other said. Then he added softly, "Unless something happens to change their attitude. . . ."

Starkey's jaded policeman's-eye soured. "Uh-huh. Idell Southworth is a nice example of attitude, by the way. Purse snatching, stomping, extortion—not to mention narcotics. Plus battery on a thirteen-year-old girl!"

He opened Idell's folder, riffled papers, and read angrily, " 'Hit her, then threatened the girl with a knife.' How do you like that for attitude, Robbins? A little girl!"

"I know. Some of them are pretty hopeless. Why did he do it?"

Starkey read on: " 'Denied using the knife. Said he didn't mean to hurt her. Just wanted her to notice him.' You're going to rehabilitate this crumb, eh?" he said.

The social worker frowned at the folders. "A kid joins a gang because he's been thrown out of every school, playground, and club in the city, Sergeant. Not one in ten has a father. He's been in trouble since he was seven or eight. When he gets to be twelve or thirteen, there's nothing left for him; nowhere to go. So he lashes up with other boys of his own stripe. *Now* they've got status! 'We're Moors! Don't get in our way, or we'll stomp you!' "

The police officer shrugged. "I'm not saying it's the kid's *fault* that he's a crumb. It's his parents that made him that way. But now he's a criminal—you can't argue that. So what are you going to do with him? Shake your finger under his nose when he beats a little girl?"

"Sometimes you can't do anything but send him to an institution. But we hope to win a boy's confidence long enough that he'll tell us when he's got a problem. Then maybe we can help him deal with it."

Starkey laughed. "I'll tell you who's got a problem, brother: you! They'll laugh you right out of the Flats."

The worker smiled. "We'll go through a testing period, all right. It probably isn't a conscious thing with them, but these boys don't trust anything but their own noses—and to them I'll smell like a policeman. They'll do everything they can to drive me out. So I leave my pride in the car when I go to a meeting with them."

The police officer sighed. "I know. I've knocked myself out time and again to help some kid I took a shine to. But now I wear my All-American Sap pin inside my undershirt. The scratching reminds me that you can't bring the dead back to life."

A telephone rang. The sergeant said, "I wish you luck, Robbins. Call on us if you need help."

For an hour, the social worker studied the files. Much of the information he already knew, from the profile of the Moors gang which the agency had been building up during the last few months. There were twelve boys in the group, thirteen if Rufus Henry were included. In age, they ranged from fifteen to twenty. Only a couple had fathers. Two boys, Whitey

James and Rufus Henry, revealed high potentials. A single member went to school regularly. Another boy attended a Saturday class in machine shop. Two other Moors had part-time jobs with the County Park Department. All had been in and out of school repeatedly, but behavioral problems and truancy had made educating them impossible. All had held jobs which they had lost for various reasons.

And so, by gravitation, they had come to rest finally at the sidewalk level, where everything was easy and everything was fun; except the one great and terrifying problem of staying alive.

As he left, the worker asked the sergeant:

"Where's a good place to start looking for these boys?"

"They hang out at the Happy Spot most of the time. Or they may be cruising in a car. If they're not cruising, they're likely to be up on the roof at Gibson's place."

It was noon. The Moors were killing time atop the Project building in which Baby lived. A chain-link fence enclosed the roof, which was tarred and graveled like a parking lot and cluttered with big boxlike ventilators and sagging clotheslines. At the far end of the roof, a young Mexican woman was hanging out wash. A baby played in a laundry basket at her feet. From the fence, Rufus could see for miles in all directions. What he saw were hundreds of buildings similar to the one on which the Moors were gathered—geometrical shapes of brown, pink, and green stucco. Southward rose the potato-shaped hills of Cathedral Heights. To the north lay the wide, shallow canyon of the river, concrete-lined and glistening with railroad tracks.

Rufus turned from the fence to gaze disconsolately

at the Moors. A great, suffocating somberness filled him. He was dull with sleeplessness, and a nervous expectancy of trouble fretted him. He watched Baby working out with his homemade barbells. The bells consisted of cans of cement fixed to an old automobile axle. Willie Clanton played a sad jazz tune on his harmonica. Idell Southworth was smoking in his special way, never releasing the smoke until it was completely absorbed by his lungs. Leeroy Purvis sat with Headshrinker, another undersized boy. Headshrinker had a very black, wizened face, and he existed in the fighting gang by acting as errand boy and court jester. Headshrinker saw Rufus gazing at him, and grinned.

"You hear ol' Bantu las' night? 'I'm going to tell you jes' like this, Sergeant: I don't use *no* kind of drugs. That the truth.' And then they find a dozen red devils in his hat!"

The sound of the boys' laughter was explosive. It faded at once. The young woman at the far end of the roof glanced over her shoulder at them and went on hanging out clothes.

"That Bantu is a sure-enough clown," Rufus said sarcastically. "He's probably clowned us right back into the joint."

Suddenly Baby nudged his arm. "Look down there an' tell me who's coming!"

The boys crowded the fence to stare down into the rectangle of grass between the buildings. Narrow cement walks traversed the grass, shiny as snail tracks. Rufus's eye was caught by a tall Negro in a business suit walking toward the building. He looked lean and purposeful and carried a folder under his arm. When the man reached the apartment house, he turned briskly toward the stairway that zigzagged upward through a series of open-air landings to the roof. In a moment they heard his heels clang on the iron treads.

"Who you reckon it is?" whispered Leeroy.

"Can't be no cop," said Willie, " 'cause we ain't done nothing. I mean since las' night—"

For some reason, all the boys looked at Rufus, as though he were the one who could give the final word on their situation. "Let's wait and see," he said. "If he asks what we're doing, just play it cool."

The stranger crossed the second-floor landing and came on, his footfalls ringing harshly. Whitey gazed anxiously at Rufus.

"How you mean, cool, man?"

"Line up here at the fence," Rufus said. "Keep your backs to the stairs. Let me do the talking." He scooped up a handful of loose gravel and leaned against the fence.

Idell, however, disdainfully swaggered to one of the ventilators and sat on the floor with his back to it, rejecting Rufus's authority. The others hesitated. But one by one they turned their backs to the roof.

Rufus heard the stranger reach the top of the stairs and stand there breathing hard from exertion. "Whee-ew! That is quite a climb!" said the man.

No one spoke; an airplane droned overhead; a horn honked on Durango Street. Presently the man's heels came crunching across the roof toward the fence. Rufus's flesh crawled. Plain-clothes man? Vice cop?

"You fellows must be the Moors," said the visitor.

Rufus opened his fist and let some gravel go spinning down the side of the building. The silence tightened. He saw Whitey chewing his lip.

"Idell, that must be a real absorbing book," the man commented. "I don't think you even heard me. By the way, my name is Alex Robbins—if anybody's interested."

Rufus released some more gravel. The stranger

came to the fence and peered over, as though curious to discover what the boys saw down there. Rufus stole a glance at him. The man had a smart and rugged brown face, the face of a linebacker who would hit you from the blind side, split you wide open, and never stop smiling. The pleasant lines beside his eyes did not fool Rufus for a moment.

"Rufus," said the man softly, "I've got nothing but time. But you fellows haven't. That big net's coming down over some of you mighty soon. Just for the record, I work with an agency called Group Service Council. We try to help boys like you. Sergeant Starkey suggested that I look you up."

Rufus cleared his throat and leaned out a little farther to spit. The others spat also.

"Well, that's my story," the man said. "I'll leave my card with Walter's mother." He walked away.

Rufus groaned. Time to talk. For any place you cut this cat, he would bleed like a cop. Under that trim coat of his, there were sure to be a gun, a badge, and a heart like a tombstone. Rufus let him reach the top of the stairs. Then he said gruffly:

"Hey, dad."

The man faced him, smiling. "Yes, lad!"

"What are you? A headshrinker or a cop?"

"Neither. I'm a social worker. I work with gangs."

"Oh, a gangbuster!"

"More of a fixer than a buster," said Alex Robbins.

Rufus peered suspiciously at the stranger, not fathoming him; not seeing any deeper than the white-toothed smile and the jolly but piercing eyes.

"What do you mean, a fixer?" Rufus demanded.

"Well, let's say a group has been getting into trouble. I try to find out why they can't stay in line like other boys. Sometimes I find they've got problems at home or in school. I go to work on these problems—

try to square things around for them. You dig?"

"Okay, Fixer," said Rufus. "Fix us up with Star-key."

"If I can, will you meet me at Walnut Street play-ground tonight?"

Rufus scratched his head. The Fixer was grinning broadly. Because he knew he had them. Whatever his racket, he could and would blow the whistle on them if they refused to play the game. To Rufus's surprise, however, Baby provided a momentary escape.

"We ain't allowed at Walnut Street," he said. "We got throwed out too many times."

"Maybe I can even fix that. Seven o'clock in the crafts room?"

Rufus heard the boys choking on their rage. They still did not realize they were in trouble up to their eyeballs; that a cat who could fix things could also unfix them. It was his game; they had to play it and like it.

"Make it eight," he said glumly.

"Eight is great," said Alex. "Or nine would be fine."

Leeroy giggled. Rufus scowled at him. The social worker gave them a salute and trotted down the stairs and out of sight.

As soon as he was gone, the gang turned on Rufus. "Are you crazy?" Idell yelled. "The Moors never had a sponsor since the beginning. Bantu will kill you!"

Rufus let them rave. Then he said: "Nobody has to go that doesn't want to. Me, I'd rather play ping-pong at Walnut Street than go back to Pine Valley. That's the choice old clownin' Bantu left us."

"Man, I hope I'm around when he hears about it!" Idell said.

"Anybody that's coming," Rufus said, "bring dark glasses. And be at the playground at a quarter till."

"How come dark glasses?" asked Whitey.

"Just an idea. I might decide to do a little fixing myself. . . ."

ELEVEN

In the evening, Rufus's mother poured coffee and milk and put a newspaper-wrapped parcel on the kitchen table. She called the children to dinner. Then she unwrapped the parcel and showed them a colorful assortment of tiny sandwiches cut in clover-leaves, crescents, and diamonds. There were several varieties of bread, and the fillings were tempting; avocado-green, pimento-pink, creamy-white with black specks of olive.

"Miz Fitzgerald give a party today," she explained, "and these was leftovers. They real good. I been eating them all afternoon while I cleaned up the kitchen mess."

What puzzled Rufus was that she had taken the Moors escapade so lightly. She had shown up at the police station to claim him like a lost dog, had signed some papers, and had escorted him home. Not a word of abuse or of correction. In the morning she had left for work before he got up.

"You hear from that p.o. of mine?" he asked, his mouth full.

"No."

Rufus picked up the newspaper, which was several

days old and had been dampened to keep the sandwiches fresh. It was the sports section. He glanced at
it, and was about to drop it when he saw a small boxed
story in a lower corner.

MARAUDERS GET ERNIE
BROWN IN BIG TRADE

Rufus caught his breath. He spread the paper on
the table to read the story.

Ernie Brown, the big Kansas City Corsairs
halfback, reports this week to the Coast City
Marauders for spring training, following a trade
between the two professional football clubs. . . .

Rufus dropped the paper on the floor. He tried to
continue eating, but his mouth had gone dry. He
could not work up enough saliva to moisten his food.
In his mind a scene unrolled like a movie:
*Ernie comes out of his house, and I'm standing
there on the walk. He starts to go by me, and I step
up so he has to look me right in the eye. "Hello,
Ernie," I say. He says, "Do I know you, boy?" I say,
"You ought to, I'm your son."*
No. I wouldn't have the guts to do it that way.
*It's after a game next fall, and the minute it's over
I jump the rail onto the field. Ernie's slogging along
with his head down and his helmet hanging in his
hand. I step in beside him and say, "Ernie, did you
ever know Etta Brown, in Leesburg, Mississippi?" And
he goes so pale he could pass for white.*
". . . Tell you who did call me, though," his mother
was saying.
Rufus looked up, unable to swallow the food and
not even knowing what she had said. He took a drink

of milk and washed it down. "What?" he said.

"Man who did call me was a social worker named Robbins."

"Who's he?"

His mother smiled. "Oh, now don't tease your mother," she said.

"How'd he find you?" Rufus asked, sullenly.

"He telephoned Miz Fitzgerald's house and left a message for me to call him. So I called soon as I quit work."

"What did you tell him?"

"I didn't tell him nothin'. Because I'm not interested no more. I wash my hands of the whole kit and caboodle. The Lord's my witness I've done all I could. But the same things goes on and on. I'm too old to think they're going to change. He say to me he's going to sponsor your group, and I say, 'You mean his *gang?*' And he say that's what he means. Not only *that,* but he wants to organize a gang of us *parents* of the Moors!"

Rufus glowered. "Parents! How come?"

"Just to talk about our problems, he tell me. Find out other people having the same problems. I tell him I knows all the hard-luck stories I need to, and I say thank you kindly, and hang up."

"Good," Rufus muttered. "I don't know who sicked him on us, but he says he's going to fix things up for us at the police station. That's why we're letting him hang around."

"He's got a lot of surprises in store for him, that man," said Mrs. Henry. "You kids going to cut up his tires and all?"

Rufus winked at Curtis. "Prob'ly." He picked up the paper. "We got a meeting with him tonight. See you later."

Upstairs, he cut out the newspaper story about

Ernie Brown and laid it on top of his scrapbook to dry. Beyond the window, darkness smothered the Flats; the pace of the freeway traffic had slowed.

Big Ernie in town! He did not yet know what he was going to do. But somehow he would find a way to get right close to Ernie, look him in the eye, and decide whether he was his father. And after that maybe he would know how to feel about it. Whether to hate him for letting them live like this while he drove Cadillacs and owned a big house, or to be proud of being his son.

Rufus followed the alleys to the north end of the playground. The big field was dark. At the far end of it he could see lights in the old mission-style buildings. Floodlights blazed under the pepper trees, where table games were being played. He heard faint yells as he scrambled over the fence and started down the field at a long-legged trot. He savored the springy, muscular action of his legs. He made a little sprint, jumped for an imaginary pass, and dodged a couple of tacklers. He stopped dead and cut right to shake the safety man. Then he went driving across the goal line.

He slowed to a walk as he passed the handball courts. Most of the boys were Negro or Mexican. He looked over the building, a two-storied lump of green plaster, pale and streaked. A leaky drinking fountain by the steps had created a small quagmire. He found the Moors loafing on the walk before the building. They turned, surprised, as he walked up.

"Where you come from?" Baby asked.

Rufus grinned. "I'm on the Gassers' most-wanted list, so I travel by the trees. Everybody here?"

"Everybody but Bantu," said Whitey. "He still in the joint."

"All you guys got glasses?"

Those who were not already wearing sunglasses pulled them from their pockets. Rufus put on a pair of glasses with heavy black frames that he had bought that afternoon. Whitey donned a pair with round white frames that, against his black face, made him look as though he were wearing a gas mask.

"How come the glasses?" he asked.

"Because if a guy can't see your eyes, he don't know what's going on in your head. We'll keep this cat wondering. Anybody got any ideas how to handle him?"

Settling his hat over one eye, Idell said: "Yeah, I got an idea. Wait till Bantu comes back."

Rufus shook his head. "Huh-uh. We've got to settle something with this so-called social worker tonight. Either he handles us or we handle him. We'll push him as far as we can without him walking out. If I see him steaming up, I'll rub my eyes. Let's go."

TWELVE

The crafts department was a small room tucked under the wide front steps. At a long masonite table, they found Alex Robbins looking over some papers. As the boys entered, he gave them that big, comradely grin.

"Right on time," he said. "Let's all find seats."

Some of the boys moved toward the table. Rufus

shook his head. He put his hands on his hips and gazed at the crafts displays around the walls.

"They got all kinds of garbage down here, ain't they?" he said.

He started moving about, jeering at the handiwork. Following his lead, the others commenced ridiculing the displays. "Oh, man, ain't that kite a panic?" "And look at this here plaster o' Paris cow! Got a face just like Simon Jones's girl friend!"

The social worker waited for a minute. As the bedlam increased, he said, "All right, fellows. Let's find chairs."

The boys glanced at Rufus. He continued moving about, hands tucked into his hip pockets. He stopped before a poster explaining tinfoil cookery.

"How to make Gasser stew," he pretended to read. "Take one Gasser, slice into quarters, and rub with garlic. Then boil rapidly until tender."

The boys shook the walls with haw-hawing laughter. Whitey started examining the kite, and tore the paper. Willie and Everett began hurdling chairs. A chair crashed over. Willie pushed Everett against the table.

"You clumsy, man! Pick it up."

Everett picked it up, but in doing so he knocked over another. More laughter. Rufus glanced covertly at Mr. Robbins, who sat poker-faced at the end of the table, toying with a pencil. Suddenly the worker began putting papers into a folder. Rufus moved to a chair at the other end of the table. He rubbed his eye, and the other boys hurried to find seats.

"I think that's everybody," the worker said. "Now, in case anybody missed it before, my name is Alex Robbins. You can call me Alex. The purpose—"

"Alex, huh?" Rufus said. "You Alexander the Great, Chief?"

"I bet he Alexander Graham Bell!" Whitey yelled.

"You the man had my old lady's telephone took out?" Idell asked.

Baby pounded the table. "No, no—he Alexander Ragtime Band!"

Willie gave his harmonica a wipe and commenced playing "Alexander's Ragtime Band." In a moment they were all singing at the tops of their voices.

Alex glanced up at the wall clock.

Hastily, Rufus rubbed his eye. In an instant the room was so silent they could hear the youngsters pla ıg outside. The worker ran his gaze around the table, but met only their blackglass stares. He frowned.

"It's your time, boys," he said. "But if I have to tell the agency tomorrow that I've struck out—well, maybe you have, too."

"What's this here *agency?*" asked Rufus meekly. "We don't dig that."

"My agency works exclusively with gangs. Once a week a worker like me gets together with the gang he's assigned to, and he and the boys talk."

"About what?"

"Problems—such as Idell's telephone being taken out. Sometimes we can help."

"That's okay about the telephone, friend," said Idell. "The Welfare people give us some signal flags. We just wigwags our friends from the roof, now."

The boys began semaphoring with their arms. Rufus shook his head, and they stopped. He was genuinely intrigued by what the worker was saying. It had to be a trap. But he needed to know how it operated in order to work around it.

"Then you really aren't a cop?" he asked.

"All I've got is what you see, Rufus—no badge, gun, or whistle."

"Then how come they dropped the charges against us?" asked Rufus, innocently.

"Because Sergeant Starkey co-operates with us when he can. Believe it or not, the police would rather have you out of jail, too."

"So you help us with our problems," Rufus said. "Is that all there is to it?"

Alex gazed at him. He was silent, and the air grew charged while they waited.

"That's only the beginning," he said. "You boys know as well as I do that you're in a jam. That's why you all swing together—because you're afraid to go it alone."

Chairs creaked as the boys reacted. Idell swore.

"Afraid, huh?" he said. "I been knifed, stomped, and slugged, daddy—and I'm still a Moor! I'll be a Moor till the night they drag me out of that alley."

"But you're a Moor because you're scared, Idell," said Alex. "Isn't that so?"

Whitey got up. "We ain't taking this garbage from no Mickey Mouse social worker!" he snapped. "Come on!"

The boys shoved their chairs back and headed for the door. Only Rufus and the worker remained at the table. Rufus peered at Alex, outraged but puzzled. What Alex had said was true. Every boy in the room knew it; that was why they were so enraged. At Pine Valley, Baby used to confide: "I got this feeling I'll never wake up, Rufe. I'm afraid to go to sleep." It was a different fear from Rufus's, who was merely afraid of being killed before he ever made it to bed.

"I wish you'd stay," Alex said seriously. "I think I can help you."

Baby Gibson glanced back from the door and saw Rufus still sitting there. He stopped, his big frame blocking the door. "Well, come on," he said, irritably.

"Wait a minute," Rufus said. "So we're scared," he said to Alex. "What's your agency do about that, if you're so good?"

"I try to find out what's wrong at home—what's wrong at school—what's wrong in general, that boys need a gang. The aim is to change your pattern of behavior. Because you know you can't go on like this."

"How are you going to change our pattern? With wienie roasts?"

Alex smiled. "We'll have outings, Rufus. It won't be all business. For the time being, just look on me as a friend. We'll talk about anything you like at our meetings—girls, school, parents—you name it."

"The only problem *we* got, Friend," said Idell, "is getting you off our backs. Can we talk about that?"

Alex laughed. "Sit down. We'll take it up as soon as we elect a president for this club."

"We already got a president," Idell retorted.

"No, I mean for our social club. Wouldn't it be a good idea to start off with duly-elected officers for the new club?"

Rufus waved his hand, and the boys came drifting back to the table. He waited until they were all seated. Then he said, "I nominate Leeroy."

Laughter broke out. It was funny but cruel, for Leeroy Purvis was undersized and sickly. Whitey put his hand on Leeroy's shoulder.

"Man, you got to be kidding." He laughed. "Ol' Leeroy would need a caddy to carry his gavel."

Leeroy grinned, and his embarrassed gaze went around the table. Rufus was the only boy not laughing. He did not want to hurt Leeroy's feelings, but it had to be done.

"It's because you've got a better record than most of us, Leeroy," he said seriously. "Look at Bantu's rap sheet. How would it be if we got rousted by the cops and they said, Who's your headman? and we had to say, Bantu. Man, we'd all be dead!"

He saw Alex frown. For Alex got the point: That's what we think of your club, Friend: I nominate a semi-invalid for president. But Alex cheerfully bounced right back, got a second to the nomination, and saw Leeroy elected. Then he asked for nominations for secretary, and Rufus chose Whitey; the gang backed him up, all except Idell, Bantu's lieutenant, who was smoking silently and glaring at Rufus. He would not forgive Rufus for acing Bantu out of the presidency. Sooner or later, maybe after Bantu came back, there would have to be an understanding between them, Rufus knew.

Alex placed a composition book and pencil before Whitey and told him to keep track of who was present at meetings and what was discussed. Rufus felt the quicksand sucking at his feet; so did the others, who looked at him to see whether he would let the worker nail them down like this. It sounded like his next suggestion would be a paper drive to buy club beanies. Before he could make up his mind how far he could go in opposing Alex, the worker dropped a bomb.

"How many of you would like to watch the Marauders football team work out some day?" he asked.

The Marauders were the team Ernie Brown had just been sold to. Rufus went on guard at once. Had Mr. Travers passed the word about his scrapbook? The Moors were all excited, now. Alex was explaining:

"I've got this friend who's a trainer for the Marauders. He can get us tickets next fall, or we can visit their training camp 'most any time. I guess you heard they've got Ernie Brown?"

"Who's he?" asked Leeroy.

Alex hooted. "Listen to the man! He's only been voted most valuable player in the National League the last two seasons! Ernie stands six-feet-six—three hundred pounds of hard-charging black man!"

"He's a tackle, ain't he?" yelled Willie Clanton.

Alex pondered a moment. "I believe he is. Yes, that's right. He plays left tackle."

Rufus snorted. "He's a halfback. And he only stands six-four, and weighs two-forty."

Alex looked embarrassed. "Are you sure?"

"You're talking to the Big Ernie expert," Baby told him. "Rufe's got a scrapbook about Ernie bigger than a telephone book."

"Is that a fact?" said Alex, looking friendly and interested.

Anger flashed across Rufus's mind. He was sorry he had contradicted the worker, for now he was certain that the Big Ernie matter had been tossed out as bait.

"What scrapbook you talking about?" he asked Baby. "Maybe that's why you were at Pine Valley, Something wrong with your head."

Bewildered, Baby scratched his neck. "I heard it a hundred times, Rufe. All you could talk about was Big Ernie—"

Alex hastily gathered his papers together. "Something wrong with my head, too, because I sure did think he was a tackle. Anyway, that's it for tonight. We'll meet here again next week, same time."

THIRTEEN

Rufus was twelve when his mother first told him about Ernie Brown. It was just after he began getting involved in serious trouble with the police.

One night, after bringing him home from the police station, she had said angrily:

"Wouldn't it make your father proud to know you was running around stealing things with them bad boys?"

Rufus sat on his bed wondering if she were going to whale him with his belt. She had promised to use the buckle end next time. The remark about his father puzzled him, though.

"Don't know whether it would or not," he muttered. "Maybe he runs around stealing things too, when he can't get them any other way."

His mother's hand slapped his mouth. "That just enough of *that,* young man! Your father steal? Huh!"

Rufus hitched away, angry and dry-eyed. "No—he was too lazy to steal," he retorted.

. . . It was the last time she ever whipped him. He was growing too large to be whipped. Rufus was puzzled that she should defend her ex-husband's reputation so vigorously, however. John Henry had been an exceptionally mean and lazy man who never held a job longer than a few months, and finally, after Curtis's birth, had disappeared for good.

His mother finished whipping Rufus and threw the belt on the bed. "Don't you never mention him again, Rufus," she said. "You don't even know who you' real father was. So how you know what he was like?"

But Rufus did mention him again. Every day for a week he questioned her about his real father.

The most fantastic possibilities crowded his mind.

If that scowling, shiftless, come-and-go father, John Henry, were not his father, who was? Someone who commanded respect, apparently. Maybe a Negro doctor, a lawyer, or a big-time jazz musician! He scrutinized pictures of famous entertainers and businessmen in the Negro magazines, trying to discover resemblances to himself. In the meantime he questioned her a dozen times a day.

One night Mrs. Henry sighed: "Rufus, listen here. If I tell you about your father, you got to promise not to tell *nobody*, never. Because nobody would believe us, and it would make us a laughingstock."

Rufus promised. Silently she handed him a sports magazine. He looked at it, puzzled.

"I found this at one of the places I works at," she said. "Look at the page I turned down. . . ."

It was a story about a Negro football player who had moved up from the minor leagues recently to join a major Eastern team. He was leading his team to the league championship his first year in the big time.

"That's your father, Rufus," Mrs. Henry said. "Ernie Brown. We was both in high school when we got married. And our folks got the marriage annulled a few months later. His folks had a little money, and he went on to college. He sent money every month until I married John Henry. After that, John Henry adopted you legal. So your real father don't have to send me money no more."

That was how Rufus learned about his father. Even now, five years later, he did not know whether to love or hate the idea of Ernie Brown. It was like a very disorderly room in his mind that he was afraid even to try to straighten up.

But this was the first time in all those years that he had dreamed of actually meeting him. He would not hold his breath waiting, however. When the chips were down, old Friend Alex would slip the hold and say his trainer-buddy had been shipped to Minneapolis, so he couldn't get them into the Marauders' training camp after all. And then he would start asking Rufus what impressions he had of his father. . . .

FOURTEEN

All the following afternoon, the Moors hung around Durango Street. They would buy something at the Happy Spot, then go stand on a street corner and watch the action. The trouble was, there was no action. Women with kids trailing them went shopping. Men drifted into the bars, prowl cars cruised the area, and cops eyeballed them as they passed. Up in Cathedral Heights it would be the same. The Gassers would be killing time waiting for trouble to offer itself, or for the right time to go looking for it.

Rufus was still one up on Simon Jones, and Simon must be planning something big, to be taking so long about it. Rufus looked over the Moors pessimistically, thinking that they would be of small help when trouble came. Bantu had let this gang go into dry rot. Like old soldiers, they relived past battles instead of planning the next one.

Darkness came. Some of the boys went home to dinner. Rufus and a few others bought malts and bowls of chili red with grease at the taco stand. Suddenly Idell said:

"I've got an idea. Let's go down to Escala Court Project and hunt Aztecs! Them beans think they got off clean shootin' out Whitey's tire that time. Let's get us some weapons and mess up a couple of 'em."

"Without Bantu?" said Whitey, dubiously.

"I don't mean throw with the whole gang—just nail a couple of loose ones. Then we'll have something to tell Bantu when he gets back."

Rufus waited for the idea to wilt; instead, it began to grow. The Moors knew better than to tackle any gang as a unit, but the idea of taking on strays excited them. "Beans" were Mexicans, and there was deep rivalry between them and Negroes. They hunched their heads together over the table and discussed it in whispers.

"All of us go?" Baby asked. "That's asking for it. The Aztecs got a communications system like the Signal Corps."

"Two or three at a time," Willie suggested.

"Whitey's right," Rufus said. "It's for the president to say when we raid. Wait till he gets back."

As he was speaking, he saw a tall youth in a mustard-colored T-shirt drift in from the street and come shambling through the empty tables. Rufus slowly laid down his spoon. Idell, sitting beside him, straightened suddenly with a sharklike grin.

"Here he come right now!" he said. "Here come the big man hisself—"

They watched the headman approach. *Big man!* thought Rufus, scornfully. Bantu's black pants and yellow shirt were dirty and wrinkled; his Tyrolean hat was crumpled. He leaned against a post and studied them with bleary eyes and a loose grin. Idell went over and slapped his shoulder.

" 'Bout time you showed up, man!" he said. "How you been, huh?"

Bantu muttered: "Gimme a butt, somebody. What's the word?"

"Good, man, now that you' back."

Idell handed him his own cigarette. Bantu drew on it, gazing at Rufus. He blew smoke at him and said:

"Man come to see me in the Hall yesterday. Claimed he was sponsoring the Moors! Now, ain't that a crock?"

Rufus saw Bantu's eye trembling, and his mouth twitched. He was charged up like a bottle of soda water. Rufus stood up.

"It's the truth, man," he said. "We've got a sponsor. We're a club, now, like the Mousketeers. Because you started a fight on that playground, where we were bound to get caught."

"We got a new president, too," Idell said nastily.

Bantu looked at him with sleepy interest. "Oh, yeah?"

Idell pointed at Leeroy. "Him," he said. "Stand up, President Purvis."

Leeroy swallowed and stood up, grinning fearfully.

Bantu blinked, then strolled over and inspected the small, chunky boy with the large eyes from which fifteen years of fear and misery looked out. Leeroy said, faintly, "Hi, Bantu."

"Congratulations, President Purvis," said Bantu. Without warning, he drove his fist into Leeroy's face. The smaller boy fell over the bench and lay on the bricks, blood pouring from his nose.

"You'll never be president of *nothin'*, the longest day you live!" Bantu shouted. "You the *nothin'* man, punk!"

Rufus came around the table. As Bantu started kicking Leeroy, Rufus threw a roundhouse right that thudded into his ear. Bantu stumbled into a latticework that screened the eating area from the side street. He staggered aside, but when he squared off to Rufus he was holding something that glittered. He squeezed it, and a steel blade shot from his hand with a click.

Rufus backed up.

Grinning viciously, Bantu followed, the switchblade probing toward Rufus.

Baby lunged up. "You hold right there," he warned Bantu. "Else I'll break your head with a bench!"

Bantu halted. "He ain't big enough to fight a man alone, huh?"

Rufus stayed on his toes, tense and ready, his stomach quivering. "I'm big enough," he said. "Let's go out in the alley and settle it. We don't need blades, either."

"Blades are a boy's best friend, Henry. You can't go against the Gassers with fists, can you? Better get in practice. Somebody give him a blade. I'll wait in the alley."

He sauntered back to the street.

Rufus looked at the others. Their eyes appraised him as if he were a secondhand car. They were his friends, but as leader he had to be more than a friend. After a moment Whitey silently handed him a knife. Rufus tossed it on his palm, then touched the button and made the blade *snick* into position. He shrugged and followed Bantu.

Bantu waited in the middle of the alley, the knife glittering in his hand. The narrow lane was somberly lit by the dull city glow reflecting off a cover of mist. On one side were the backs of stores; on the other, a line of reeling back-yard fences. The boys formed a loose ring to enclose Rufus and the gang leader.

Rufus watched Bantu twist the knife as though he were coring an apple. Bantu's head sank lower and he shuffled toward Rufus an inch at a time, his free hand moving delicately like that of a fencer. Rufus gave ground. The knife in his own hand bothered him more than Bantu's. If he killed Bantu, he would go back to prison for good. He might even get the gas chamber. If he merely cut him up, he would surely go back to jail if word got out who had done the cutting.

Suddenly he tossed the knife away.

Bantu straightened, smiling broadly. "Quittin' just in time, nigger," he said. "I could see a big smile across your Adam's apple, like it'd been cut there."

"Who needs a knife?" Rufus retorted. "You'll look like I'd used a cleaver, time I get through."

Bantu lunged in and slashed at his stomach. Rufus jumped back. Bantu was slow; he smelled of liquor. He made another pass, and Rufus clutched at his wrist. But the headman slipped the hold, and the knife creased Rufus's forearm. He felt the flesh open painlessly. Then it began to burn like an ant sting, and the blood scalded him as it poured from the wound.

"Bleed like any nigger, don't you?" Bantu taunted.

Rufus pretended to look at the cut, and backed away. But when Bantu started to follow, Rufus stopped, slashed at the headman's jaw, and danced back out of range. He missed by an inch. Bantu took a wild swipe at the spot where Rufus's fist had been. The pass was a foot short, and he finished off balance. Rufus stepped forward and banged a solid hook into the side of Bantu's head. The headman staggered. Rufus hit him on the jaw with a left, on the nose with a right, and Bantu was blinded by tears of pain. Rufus raised his fist like a hammer and smashed it down on the other's wrist.

The knife fell to the pavement.

Bantu stared at the weapon, dazed, then squatted suddenly to recover it. Rufus put his foot on the knife. Bantu came up like a spring, ramming his head into Rufus's abdomen, but Rufus slashed lefts and rights into the side of Bantu's head until he fell. Bantu rested there on all fours, hurt and befuddled.

There was a murmur of pleasure from the boys watching the struggle. *You get beat' into the gang, and you get beat' out.* All of them had been beaten on Bantu's orders when they became Moors. Now he owed them the same kind of show.

He got up slowly, scraping up the last of his energies, and went after Rufus with his head lowered. Rufus picked off his swings and jarred him with hooks to the sides of his head. The headman kept coming, while his eyes puffed closed and his bloody lips swelled. At last he was leaning forward as though he were boring in, but all that kept him from falling was Rufus's fists.

Rufus let him fall. Bantu lay there half conscious. He crawled a foot at a time to the edge of the alley and lay close to the brick wall.

Baby slapped Rufus on the back. Whitey gripped his hand. They were pounding him and telling him he was the headman now. His arm burned, and he was sick with the reaction from fear and anger. He felt as though he were about to throw up. But he looked around, feigning calmness.

"Idell, man," he said, "see if he's got any money in his pockets. He owes me half my gate money."

"Sure, man."

Idell searched Bantu's pockets and handed Rufus some coins and bills. There was eight dollars left.

"Get your car," Rufus told Whitey, "and take him home. I don't want him found here. Meeting tomorrow at my place—ten o'clock."

FIFTEEN

A hot pulsing in his arm wakened Rufus. He had cleansed the knife cut with soap and water last night and bandaged it. In the bathroom, he examined it gingerly. The wound was still oozing serum and blood. He knew a doctor should look at it, but that meant going over to the clinic at General Hospital and answering a lot of questions about what had happened.

He cleaned it again, laid a folded strip of rag over it, and taped it in place. Looking at his skinned knuckles, he smiled. He threw some imaginary punches at his reflection in the soapy mirror.

Maybe I'll go into pro boxing, he told himself. Fight under the name of Black Panther. Fastest member of the giant cat family.

Old Bantu. Poor slob didn't know he'd outgrown

his own gang. Guys did outgrow gangs. They no longer needed the gang for protection, because they were
old enough that younger boys left them alone. Finally
they dropped out. But a cat like Bantu might try to
hang onto a gang, and then somebody had to take
him out of it.

He dropped downstairs through the dark spiral
staircase, strong and eager. The old house was empty.
The kitchen clock, clicking like an infernal machine,
showed nine-thirty. Putting on water for coffee, Rufus thought of what he would tell the Moors. It was his
job to give them pride and build up their confidence.
He would forge them into a weapon that other gangs
would fear and respect.

He frowned, envisioning a problem.

They would want to know how they could remain
a fighting gang, now that they had Alex spying on
them. That was a hard one to explain, even to himself. But Rule One was that a fighting gang had to
fight, at least until it had carved out a territory no
other gang dared set foot in. By a little action now, he
could avoid action later on. He did not enjoy fighting,
but the big lesson, which do-gooders like Alex and
hard-nosed cops like Starkey did not understand, was
that you *had* to fight to stay alive.

Idell was the first boy to arrive. He came in ducking his head and grinning, looking around the dim
parlor and saying he liked a house better than an
apartment. Rufus was cold to him. He saw him begin
to perspire. Idell had backed the losing candidate,
and now he did not know where he stood.

A car drove up. Baby, Whitey, and five others
came in. The remaining four gang members arrived
afoot. They sat around on the broken furniture or
squatted on the floor, smoking and talking about the
fight.

"You got a real nice pad here," Whitey said. He was dressed sharper than usual and his long hair was neatly greased down.

"Kind of smells like somebody used to raise mushrooms under the rug, though," Rufus commented.

"Well," Baby said, beaming, "you the new president of the Moors."

Rufus winked. "No, no, *Leeroy's* the president. I'm just the secretary of war."

They laughed and joked about President Purvis. Then it was awkwardly quiet. Rufus looked at Idell in a special way.

"Idell, man, you haven't said whether you swing with me or not," he said curiously. "I know you were tight with Bantu. So how about it?"

"Well, uh, uh," Idell said uncomfortably. "Well, sure, man, but I mean—"

"I'll suspend the rule about guys getting beat out of the gang, if that's what's bothering you," Rufus said. "But walk out right now if you're going to, before we start making plans for the new Moors. I figure you've got heart, though. Be glad to have you stay."

Idell's long, hungry features relaxed. "I didn't think you'd want me, Rufe, because I was his lieutenant and all. But I swing with you now. All the way."

Rufus nodded. "Nobody that stays with me will be sorry. After I get finished, you'll be able to walk through the Heights alone, and guys that hate your guts will say, 'How you, man? Glad to see you.' They won't lay a finger on you. That's a little different from the way it is now, huh? Guys come and go in our beat like it was the Greyhound bus station."

"Oh, it ain't that bad," Whitey protested.

"It's not, huh? The Gassers are all over the Flats, and the Aztecs shoot out your tires—that's how bad it is. Why kid yourselves? A gang's no better than the leader, and Bantu was nothing."

"How you figure to straighten it out?" asked Idell.

Rufus linked his hands behind his head. They were watching him intently, chewing fingernails, smoking nervously. Willie kept flicking out the blade of his knife and pushing it back. The Moors were committed to following him, now; depending on how good a general he was, they were either on the road to the reformatory or to their old supremacy of the sidewalk.

"First," he said, "I got to get a picture in my mind of our whole beat. What streets dead-end—where to hide—all that stuff. Then we got to check our weapons and see what we need. For a while we'll have to stick close together, because sooner or later Jones is coming down here. When he sticks his nose into the Flats again, we'll bang it so hard it'll be a dimple."

Idell cleared his throat. "Yeah, but ain't we going to get busted the first time there's a fight?"

"Not if we've got witnesses that we were somewhere else when it happened."

"We ain't got any witnesses. Not that I knows of."

"If all the Flats gangs backed each other up, we'd have witnesses," Rufus declared.

Baby wrinkled his nose. "The other cats down here is all punks."

"What gangs are there?"

"There's the Aztecs," said Whitey. "They're beans —the ones that shot up my car. The only other gang, except the Little Warriors, is the Bloods. They're colored boys, and they're rough."

"Where do these gangs hang out?"

"In Escala Court Projeck. The Bloods are usually at Pelican Smith's pad. He's their headman. The Aztecs will be anyplace there's weed to smoke."

"Pick me up at eight o'clock tonight," Rufus said.

"You and I and Baby are going to talk to them about a treaty."

The Moors looked at each other. Idell raised his hands. "Take it easy, man! Escala Court is their *beat!* You don't go in there—not if you got any idea about coming out."

"We're going in," Rufus said, "and we're coming out. I'll see you tonight," he told Whitey. "And relax. We aren't going to fight—just talk."

The Moors left, heads down and shuffling. Rufus maintained his cheerful front until they were gone. Then he went up and sat on his bed and felt his heart pound. Had he moved too fast? No: when you were already behind, fast was the only way to travel. What would Big Ernie do if it were the last two minutes of the fourth quarter, and the team was a touchdown behind? He would put his head down like a bull, and charge. So that's what the son of Big Ernie was going to do.

SIXTEEN

Whitey parked under a black-trunked magnolia tree in a desolate neighborhood of crumbling California bungalows. The damp night air was bitter with smog. A few blocks east, the boxy silhouette of Escala Court Project rose above the trees.

"There's one more cross street," Whitey said. "Then the street dead-ends. Pelican lives in the last house on the right."

"If we drive in, Rufe," Baby said, "we won't drive out till Pelican pushes the button. They blocks the street with a car when anybody goes in."

"It's their playpen. Let 'em play their games."

His face somber, Whitey swung from the curb. They crossed the intersection. Half-dead magnolias, strangling in the poisonous city air, lined the street. At the end of the block was a white barricade studded with red reflectors. Rufus saw cigarettes glowing in the shadows of a porch. The house was small and tattered. In the darkness, he made out several boys sitting on the porch steps. He reached over and pressed the horn ring. The horn emitted a gentle mooing sound. The boys on the porch did not stir. He leaned out.

"I'm looking for Pelican Smith."

There was no answer.

"I'm Rufus Henry, headman of the Moors."

"Why don't you stand under the streetlight, Henry, so I can see you?" a voice called back.

Rufus stood on the sidewalk. A car without lights coasted from a driveway into the street and blocked it. Four Negro youths sauntered from the porch. Older than any of the Moors, they were slow-moving and solemn. A boy with a black shirt, black jeans, and small black hat moved around Rufus, examining him like one strange dog checking another.

"What happened to ol' Bantu?" he said.

Rufus rubbed his chin. "He turned in his uniform last night. Said he was getting too old for games."

"I heard about it," said Pelican. "What's on your mind?"

"I got a proposition to make."

"I'll make you one, Henry. Get out of here fast, and I'll forget you was ever here."

"I'm leaving, brothers," Rufus said. "Just asking a minute of your time. Seems to me all of us blood brothers ought to help each other against the Heights gangs, though. One fight, all fight."

Pelican nudged another youth. "He say he can fight! Do he look like it to you?"

"He look like a little old nigger kid with a big mouth," the other said.

"I'm not looking for a fight," Rufus said. "But if Jones shoves me up against the wall again, I'll bet I work up a good sweat."

"Maybe you better sweat some more over him, Henry, before you come around telling us how good you are. I hear he's looking for you."

"I know. That's my problem. 'Cause you know how it goes: whether you beat the other guy or not, the cops will make you look like a loser. That's unless you can prove you were someplace else."

"I guess you a loser, then, man."

Rufus grinned. "Not if some of my blood brothers will swear I was with them on the Big Lawn when it happened."

Pelican grunted. "Man, ain't my neck long enough now without sticking it out for you?"

"But, look!" Rufus argued: "Next time *you* get in a bind, I'll stick mine out for you!"

Pelican shoved his hands under his belt. He rocked back and forth on his heels. For a moment Rufus was hopeful. Then the other boy said:

"You stuck it out plenty when you come in here. But I'll forget it if you get out of sight fast enough."

"You're the boss," Rufus said. He turned and got back into the car. Up the street, the dark automobile moved back into the driveway. Whitey made a U-turn and drove off. "Uh!" he grunted, as though he had just been kicked in the stomach.

"Okay, let's hunt up the Aztecs," said Rufus. He was perspiring.

"Man, listen to me!" Baby pleaded. "We just got out of there alive, and you better believe it. Now, these here Aztecs may be small, but they mean as red ants. They were in a shooting mess last year. Their old president is doin' hard time at Deuell."

"They won't hurt us. No reason to."

Baby groaned. Whitey shook his head hopelessly and turned east across the Flats. Rufus wet his dry lips. He was started now; had to keep driving. They drove through the curving streets of another housing project. Dry sycamore leaves, brown and thin as paper, crunched under the tires. Set back from the walks, the big, sad-looking apartment buildings rose square and graceless as concrete blocks. Whitey stopped before a building that looked exactly like all the rest.

"A kid named Tojo's their headman," he said. "He might be in that courtyard between the buildings."

In this narrow space Rufus made out scrubby trees, trash barrels, and gas meters. He had stayed alive this long by keeping out of such places. But you had to talk to people where they were.

"I'll go alone this time," he said.

"No. We'll all go," Baby said.

They advanced boldly across the beaten-down lawn. Bits of broken glass crunched underfoot, glints of it sparkling everywhere. From the freeway came a bass booming of trucks. As they reached a roadblock of trash barrels at the entrance to the narrow courtyard, there was a loud metallic pop. Rufus knew the sound: someone who had been sitting on a trash barrel had stood up, letting the lid pop back into shape.

"Anybody here named Tojo?" he called.

He imagined he could hear them breathing. He smelled cigarette smoke. "We're Moors," he said.

"I'm headman in Durango now, and I want to talk to Tojo."

"You' talkin' to him, cat," a Mexican voice said.

Rufus crossed his arms. "Pleased to meet you, Tojo."

"Talk," said the Mexican boy. "That's what you said, ain't it?"

As Rufus explained his Big Lawn plan, six boys filtered from their hiding places and gathered across the trash barrels from the Moors. All were small and wiry and dressed in hand-me-down clothing. All were utterly bald. Their shaven skulls caught gleams of light. A boy in the middle stood with his hands on his hips. He had a sunken chest and wore a red shirt with the sleeves chopped off at the shoulders.

"What do you say?" Rufus asked.

"I say, *chale*," Tojo said. "Take off."

"Think it over. Tell me tomorrow. You can usually find us at the taco stand."

"We'll find ourselves in jail, if we lie to the cops. Why should we do that for a bunch of nig—"

The Moors straightened at the sound of the trigger word.

Tojo smiled. "Esscuse me, brothers. I meant bloods."

Rufus rocked his head. "That's all right, grease-balls—Esscuse *me*: I mean Spanish-Americans."

"Mexicans," Tojo snapped.

"Sure, man," Rufus said. "Well, if you beans change your minds, you know where to find us. But don't come into Durango unless you're ready to talk business. *Adiós,* huh?"

"*Al recle,*" Tojo said softly.

As they reached the car, a bottle crashed on the walk beside the car and splattered their ankles with fragments. They turned, but the Aztecs were hidden behind trees.

"Them lousy spicks!" Whitey choked. "Let's get the others and come back."

Rufus opened the door. He felt tired and disgusted. "Get in. If they'd meant business, they could have taken us before. We struck out. Next time they come to us."

They drove back, silent, glad to be out of the enemy's country. When they arrived at the house on Teagarden Street, a small foreign car was parked at the curb.

"It's that social worker's car," Rufus muttered. "I saw it at the playground."

"Maybe he brought your mama a basket of food," Baby joked.

"Or some old shoes for the family," Whitey suggested.

Rufus was nettled. He meant to keep the Mickey Mouse department of his life completely separate from the rest of it. He would have to straighten the worker out on coming here without telling him.

"How'd you like an old shoe in the teeth?" he said. He got out, slammed the door, and went up the walk. Whitey drove away.

SEVENTEEN

Rufus entered quietly. From the vestibule, he could see his family sitting on the swaybacked sofa, while Alex Robbins hunched on a lumpy hassock and spoke earnestly to Mrs. Henry. His coat was off, and his white shirt was the brightest thing in the parlor.

"I'd be pleased to handle it for you, Mrs. Henry," he was saying. "It would be no trouble to call the division commander and have the boys brought in for questioning."

"What boys is that?" Rufus asked, as he stepped into the room.

They all looked around, surprised. The worker said gravely: "Hello, Rufus. I dropped in to talk to your mother about the parents' group, and kind of walked into a situation."

"Oh, yeah?" Rufus said. He looked at his mother, who was frowning at a dishtowel she was knotting in her lap. "What's going on?" he asked.

Janet rose and started from the room. Rufus saw something that shocked him: one of her pigtails had been cut off. As she hurried toward the hall, he caught her arm.

"What happened, Janet? Who cut off your pigtail?"

The girl sobbed and turned her face away. But Rufus saw the bloody scrape on her cheekbone and the hard swelling under her eye. She ran on down the hall. Rufus turned to Curtis.

"What happened to her?"

"It was those dirty Gassers, that chased you and her before!" Curtis blurted. "They caught her and cut off her pigtail. Simon tied it to his car aerial. Somebody tripped her when she started to run."

A black violence rose in Rufus. Pain, sadness, and rage choked him. He started to leave the room, but Alex came quickly to his feet.

"Wait a minute, Rufus. I know where you're going, and I don't blame you. But I can't let you do it."

Rufus confronted him. "Sure—talk to the division commander, man! Have him pass the word to Simon to lay off. Then they'll come over and beat both kids half to death. You full of great ideas, aren't you?"

Alex walked toward him, tall and narrow-hipped. His hands were huge, the hands of a pass-catching end. He still maintained that irritating calmness, but the cop in him was close to the surface now. Soon the mask would drop.

"So you want Jones to go scot free," he said. "That's just fine. And that's what it will amount to if a complaint isn't filed."

Mrs. Henry objected, her face dolorous. "Mr. Robbins, I never yet won no prizes dealing with the police. Far back as I can remember, some policeman or welfare worker was criticizing the way I raised my chil'ren or didn't pay my bills. Black folks does best when they stays *out* of police stations, *whatever* they problems."

"Black isn't high fashion," Alex agreed. "But we've got to help ourselves as much as we can. The police say we're clannish—that we like to settle our own problems. Can you blame them, when we won't report a crime or testify to one?"

Mrs. Henry made some mournful sounds, and went into the kitchen. Alex picked up some papers from the floor by the hassock. "Walk out to the car with me, Rufus," he said.

They walked outside. Rufus stood on the sidewalk with him. Alex looked at him silently, until Rufus exploded:

"If you're asking me to sit still for them beating up my sister, then you're crazier than I thought!"

"And if you think you can do any good by going to war with Simon, Rufus, you're out of your mind. Fight Two grows out of Fight One. Fight Three grows out of Fight Two. Where does it stop? Sometimes at the gas chamber. Sometimes merely at the reformatory."

"Where does it stop if a guy doesn't fight back? He gets beat' until he's ready to salute every time they pass him. Me, I'll take the gas chamber."

"Well, you're going about it just right, then," Alex said. "You're a smart boy, Rufus, but you've got to use that brain God gave you. You've got to read the writing on the wall. There *is* another way to handle these things."

"Tell me about it," Rufus said.

"Simon's already on parole. I'll drop the word to him that the next time he gets out of line, he'll go to placement."

"Not without witnesses against him, and who's going to testify?"

"The arresting officers. Evidence? A weapon in his car—liquor or pills in his possession. He can be racked up."

Rufus gave the worker a broad Uncle Tom smile. "Tell you what, Mr. Robbins. You tackle him your way, I'll tackle him mine. One of us is sure to get him. Ain't that so?"

The worker raised and dropped his hands. "You've got my telephone number, Rufus. Call me from the police station. I'll bring you over some hard candy and a comic book. Comic book ought to be just right for a guy that can't use his head."

Rufus watched him drive down the street, his wheels stirring up a whirlwind of dry leaves. He snorted. They were all the same, these social worker cats. They couldn't see the real picture even when they were standing right inside it.

His mind had run ahead of him while he was arguing with Mr. Robbins, coolly delving into ways and means of dealing with Simon. It had its eye on that pigtail tied to Simon's car aerial, and it knew that there was something just right for Simon, something he would understand.

In his room, he placed on the bed the fiberboard suitcase he had brought from camp. From a nest of underwear and socks, he lifted out a portable radio, bought secondhand at the Salvation Army store two years ago. He had not plugged it in because it no longer worked. Now, with the edge of a dime, he turned two screws in the back and raised the cover. He smiled, and made a sound of content.

There they lay, in a snug bed of cleaning tissues— an even dozen dynamite caps filched from the explosives supply when they were blasting for the road.

He held one in his hand, gazing out the window at the freeway traffic charging by his window in a cat-howling fury. He stood pondering exactly how to proceed. At last he made up his mind. He closed the radio again and put it away.

Old Simon hadn't known what he was biting off. Now he had himself booked to go fifteen rounds with the Black Panther, in a ring where the bell was broken and they fought with clubs.

EIGHTEEN

In the morning, he walked his brother and sister to school. He wore a bleached-blue camp shirt with long sleeves to hide the bandage on his arm. Janet had re-arranged her hair in a knot at the back of her head to hide the loss of her pigtail. She told Rufus she felt all right. "Except I've got a little headache," she said.

"Lemme tell you about headaches," Rufus said. "Ol' Simon Jones is going to have one so big a bucket wouldn't carry it. He won't bother you any more. That's a promise."

"Rufus, don't fight them. They'll leave us alone now that they got back on you."

Rufus shook his head. "You don't know these cats. If that was true, maybe I'd rock along and see what happened. But the way it works is—the more they get away with, the more they crowd their luck. So I've got to show Simon his luck's just gone bad."

A number of Moors were already at the taco stand. Whitey and Baby Gibson were giving them the word on the visit to Escala Court last night. No one seemed surprised. Then Rufus told them about the Gassers' mistreating Janet.

There was an angry hubbub of muttered mayhem. Willie brandished his knife and threatened to shave Simon's red head. The threats were fierce and un-realistic. The truth was that the Moors were afraid. They were merely racing their engines.

When they began to cool off, Rufus said, "Tonight's the night."

They went silent, staring at him blankly.

". . . Tonight?" Willie said.

"I can see you're set to move right now," Rufus said ironically, "but it'll take a while to get ready. We'll hit them tonight."

Idell swallowed. "Blades?" he asked.

"Sure, blades!" Baby retorted. "Send Leeroy up to tell 'em it's blades, Rufe. How about we meet 'em under the freeway?"

"I'm talking about throwing, not debating," Rufus said. "If we talk terms with them, we'll haggle for a week over what we're going to fight with, and end up not fighting at all."

"I was just thinking," Whitey said, dubiously. "What's Alex going to say if we mess up?"

"Lemme tell you about him. You've seen those preachers on street corners with a little folding organ? Everybody laughs at them, but they keep on preaching. That's Alex. Whatever we do, he'll keep on preaching."

No one else appeared sure of it. Willie worried a breadcrumb on the table with his fingernail, his brow wrinkled. "Unless he's really a cop," he said.

"I had a talk with him last night. He's no cop. He's just trying to psych us. Don't worry about him. . . ." Yet he thought of the other man he had seemed to see behind Alex's eyes once or twice, and he wondered. He was seldom wrong about a person, and his first guess at Alex was that under his grin he was as hard as brass knuckles.

"I guess you right," Idell said, dubiously. "How you want to do this, man?"

Rufus explained his battle plan. First they looked doubtful, then interested, then enthusiastic. Their confidence soared. There was only a small risk in the scheme—if something did not go wrong.

"Me and Whitey are going out and pick the spot now," he said. "Best if we aren't all seen together. Word travels."

He remembered the view from the Durango Street bridge the day Mr. Travers brought him home. The concrete riverbed below, a high sloping bank on the Flats side. There was a gas storage tank at the end of the Flats, near the bank, and some vacant land.

They got into the car and Whitey headed north toward the bridge, then east up River Street, which ran precariously along the bank. Cross streets dead-ended at a barricade of stubby white posts on the left. Finally the street ended at the big storage tank and a right-of-way fence. The freeway rose just beyond.

Rufus got out and looked the ground over. Near the fence were two small sheds in a wilderness of rain-wrecked cartons and old tires. A dirt lane led down from Durango Project. There were no houses or build-ings within a quarter mile.

They went back to the taco stand, and the Moors huddled over the table while Rufus drew a map of the area, explaining how the fight would go and what was expected of each member. He told Idell and Baby to steal a hose somewhere and cut it up for clubs. "Fill the pieces with sand?" Idell asked.

"No sand. Classed as a deadly weapon, and we're going to have surprise on our side anyway."

They threw a lot of questions at him, and he calm-ly explained everything. He was pleased with the way they grasped the general idea of the raid. Yet he was sure of none of them, actually, except that they had fumbled around like a gang of mumbling stir-bugs that night when they beat him into the gang. But that was under Bantu's leadership. This would be different.

It had better be different, he thought, with a dry-ness in his mouth, or their first throw would be a disaster.

Nine-thirty P.M.

Traffic had dwindled to a few cars ambling up and down Durango. In this end of town people worked hard, weekdays, and they went to bed early. On Fri-day and Saturday nights many got drunk, fought in taverns, and wrecked their automobiles. Cathedral

Division police operated on a fourteen-car plan instead of the usual ten-car plan.

Rufus and Whitey drove slowly up Durango toward the Heights. They passed beneath the freeway. Just beyond, the street tilted steeply, paved with red bricks polished by fifty years of spinning tires and oil drippings. Three blocks farther, it leveled off. They were in a business district cast from the same mold as the Flats: a few mama-and-papa grocery stores; tiny churches with big names like the Two-Seeds-in-the-Spirit Predestinarian Baptist Church; mean little bars like sea caves; and liquor stores that were regularly held up.

"They likely be at Fat Boy's," Whitey said. "It's a drive-in. There's no car-hops any more because guys bothered them so much."

"You got everything clear, now?" Rufus asked, tensely. "Because there'll be no stopping once we've started."

"Yeah. But it's sure complicated, Rufe," Whitey muttered. "Man, if we miss by two seconds we're burned! And I don't like Leeroy having such an important job."

Rufus's eye was caught by a tall Negro youth leaning against a lamppost before a corner bar. The boy was watching their car.

"Who's that cat on the corner?" he asked quickly.

Whitey looked, and made a sound of chagrin. "Shankman! He's one of Simon's stakeouts."

Rufus was angry. "Why didn't you tell me he uses stakeouts?"

"He don't always. If Shankman goes inside that bar, it means he's recognized the car. There's an outside phone booth at the Fat Boy's, and Simon parks near it to take his calls."

The boy, a lean youth in a plastic car coat, suddenly turned and hurried into the bar.

Whitey groaned. "That's it! We'll have to call it off. Better get out of sight, too. They just as likely to come looking for us."

Rufus bit his lip, thinking sharp and hard. "How far is it to the drive-in?"

"Couple of blocks."

"Gun it!"

"Now? Simon prob'ly walking into that phone booth this minute!"

Rufus stamped hard on Whitey's gas-foot. The car lunged ahead. Whitey sat up straight and began driving. Two blocks farther, he pulled to the curb.

"That's Fat Boy's—across the next intersection."

Rufus studied the drive-in. It consisted of a sheet-metal box with screened windows where food was sold, and space for parking. A big lighted sign on top of the stand depicted a fat boy in checkered pants eating a hamburger. There was a telephone booth next to the sidewalk. The gunmetal sedan was parked beside it. As they watched, the driver's door of the sedan opened and Simon Jones slipped out. He moved to the telephone booth at his high-shouldered strut.

Rufus jumped out. "Make a U-turn and park across the street. Keep the engine running and open my door when you see me coming."

He walked quickly to the corner. In the light of the telephone booth, Simon's red hair was high and stiff. He wore a long corduroy coat, black pants, and a white muffler. Rufus saw something tied to Simon's car aerial, a little black streamer tied with a red ribbon: Janet's pigtail.

He stepped into the street, watching the other boys in the car. They seemed unsuspecting of trouble.

Head down, he crossed the street and approached the booth. Simon suddenly hung up the receiver and turned to leave.

Rufus sprinted, reaching the booth just as Simon opened the folding glass door. Rufus put his hands on the sides of the door and blocked the way.

"Hi, there, yella fella," he said, grinning.

Simon stared, his jaw hanging. Then he tried to cock his right arm for a swing; his elbow hit the side of the booth, and the blow became a nervous little jab. Rufus slapped it down. He drove a hard overhand punch to Simon's mouth. The Gasser slumped onto his hams with blood on his lips.

A boy yelled something in a high voice. Rufus turned as the first boy leaped upon him. It was Dukie. He drove his fist into Dukie's stomach, and the boy's breath went out in a pained gasp. Rufus rabbit-punched him and took off running as the whole carful of boys streamed after him.

NINETEEN

Halfway to the car, the boys realized two things: that they could never catch him and that a car was waiting for him. Two boys followed him while the others turned back to their own car. Whitey howled encouragement, as Rufus sprinted, his knees lifting high. The car started coasting and Rufus jumped in. Whitey stepped on the gas.

When they had gone a block, Rufus saw the sedan come skidding into Durango. Hands clenching the wheel, Whitey headed down the street. They clattered under the freeway arches and were in the Flats.

"You got the turns in mind, now?" Rufus yelled.

Whitey nodded. He hit the brake and cramped the wheel. They lurched into one of the grass-lined drives sweeping in graceful curves through the trash and corruption of the Project. They had five blocks to go.

At the next intersection, Whitey braked again and turned left. This street ended at the barricade.

Halfway down the block, the interior of the car was illuminated by headlights behind them. Rufus looked around. The Gassers were closing in remorselessly. A block from the dead end, the driver got on Whitey's bumper and began jarring at it as though to climb right over the car. They could hear the gang shouting. Whitey looked terrified.

"You're doing good," Rufus panted. He squeezed his hands together in an agony of nervousness.

They flashed through a final cross street. The black-top ended. The car dropped a wheel into a pothole, and the frame came down on the axle with an impact that snapped their necks. Whitey steered the car down the wandering lane between heaps of junk and sheds. The red reflectors of the barricade gleamed a hundred feet ahead.

Whitey reached for the emergency brake, and Rufus shoved his feet against the floorboards. The car fishtailed and stopped. A churning dust cloud engulfed it. The boys leaped out.

Seconds later, the Gassers pulled up with a roar of power and skidding tires.

The Heights gang stumbled from the car and charged after the fleeing Moors. Rufus passed between two ruined sheds. As he did so, he took a single high, skipping stride—like a young deer, full of life, frisking a little. Whitey gave a similar jump at the same place. Both ran on, sprinting across a stretch of bare ground to the chain-link fence beside the freeway. Reaching the fence, Rufus started to climb, but fell back and sprawled in the dirt.

"We got 'em!" Simon Jones shouted.

His shout ended in a grunt of surprise and pain. He had fallen full-length in the dirt, like a plank. A moment later Dukie went down. The tall boy called Shankman tried to swerve around them, but he, too, was cut down by the mysterious force that haunted the space between the sheds. Two more youths collapsed before Dukie sat up and screamed:

"They's a wire stretched across here!"

In one of the sheds, Baby Gibson was watching Rufus. Rufus started back. Baby turned to Leeroy, in the darkness. "Okay!"

Leeroy knelt on the dirt floor in an agony of tension. It was the most important job of his life. Between his knees he gripped a battery Rufus had purchased that day. One wire was attached to the corner terminal of the battery. Leeroy touched a wire to the other terminal, and there was a sharp *bang!* outside. Then he touched another wire to the terminal, and again there was a sharp explosion.

At the door, Baby, Willie, Headshrinker, and the others were roaring with laughter. Outside, as the dynamite caps exploded beneath the surface of the ground, the Gassers were in panic.

"They got a gun!" someone shrieked.

The air was dense with smoke and flying particles of earth. The Gassers milled, then headed back to the car.

Rufus gave the signal to attack.

The Moors rushed from the sheds upon the disorganized Heights gang, smashing, shouting, stomping the ones who fell. The fight, like all fights, immediately became a nightmare of confusion and fear. The fear was of a cat named Death, who was always in there with his glittering blade and his bitter smile. No one ever saw him; yet it was known for sure that he never missed a street fight, for all too often he left his calling card: a body.

In the dust and darkness, the Moors battled savagely. The shattered Gassers stumbled back to the cars. Baby picked up one of the downed battlers and heaved him, like a log, into the others. The boys broke and ran for the car. As they reached it, Rufus bawled:

"Look out—it's booby-trapped!"

The boys who were about to pile into it hesitated. As the Moors whipped at their heads and shoulders with their plastic-hose clubs, the Gassers ran down the dirt lane toward the Project.

Rufus charged upon the boy who was still down. The youth rose dazedly and swung at Rufus's head. It was Simon Jones. Rufus ducked his swing and caught him on the chin with a punch. Simon fell and lay stirring slowly until Baby and Headshrinker came over.

"Set him on his feet," Rufus said.

Baby hauled him up. The Moors surrounded Simon. An open cut on his cheek was clotted with blood and earth. Beneath his eye was a swelling. His lips were puffed.

Rufus stepped close. "You hear me, man?" he asked.

Wiping blood from his mouth, Simon stared at him.

"I should have warned you," Rufus said. "My best is none too good, and having my sister beat' brings out the worst in me. I'm going to say this just once, now: ever you lay a hand on my brother or sister, I'll kill you."

Simon blinked, his eyes dull.

"The Flats are changing," Rufus said. "It's not going to be the back yard you used to prowl like a tomcat. Even the *dirt's* different down here. It blows up when you step on it. You need to know where to step, see? And the right place for you to step is *out*. And that's now. You got ten minutes to get out of the Flats."

Simon staggered drunkenly toward his car.

"No, no, man," Rufus said in patient reproof. "Leave the car. That's spoils of war."

Simon's hand wearily dropped from the door handle. Without looking around, he shambled up the dark street.

As soon as the gang leader was out of sight, Whitey started the car and drove it to the barricade at the end of the street. The boys all trotted alongside. Whitey set the brake, switched off the lights, and jumped out. High on the success of their attack, the Moors set to work removing one of the posts they had loosened earlier that day. Lifted out, it left a gap between the remaining posts.

Rufus stood on the curb studying the dark riverbed. Far out in the darkness, a passenger train glided along, boatlike, with dimly lit windows. The boys were making a lot of noise, laughing and punching each other.

"Everybody know what he's supposed to do now?" Rufus said.

Leeroy bobbed his head. "Go home to bed."

"If anybody comes asking questions, you were on the Big Lawn tonight. No matter what they ask, that's all you know. You were on the Big Lawn all evening."

He got in the car, leaving the door open. The upholstery was an expensive tuck-and-roll job, soft as a woman's lap. Old Simon had a lot of money tied up in this car. Rufus backed up about fifty feet. Leaving the engine idling, he slowly let in the clutch. The car moved along at a walking pace. He sat on the outer edge of the seat with one foot already out of the car. In the darkness, the Moors danced up and down with excitement. Purring quietly, the sedan rolled closer and closer to the dead end.

Rufus yanked the hand throttle out. The engine roared. He was not expecting such quick response. As the car shot forward, he went spinning into the street. He fell, pulled his legs up and lay huddled there until the rear wheel passed.

Shaken, he sat up and stared after it.

The automobile bounced over the curb and rushed on, the roar of its engine rising to a shriek as the driving wheels lost contact with the pavement. For a moment it balanced, then toppled forward.

Headlong, it roared down the steep concrete ramp. Halfway to the bottom, the front wheels locked. The car swerved, tipped over, and with a monstrous clashing noise went rolling to the foot of the incline. Glass jangled and fenders ripped loose. As it came to rest, a flickering yellow flame like a pilot light began to glow in the wreckage. Then there was a soft explosion, and the car was engulfed in flame.

Rufus turned. The boys were out of their minds with delight. He told them sharply:

"Take off, now! Get rid of those clubs on the way. The cops will be here in a couple of minutes."

TWENTY

Shortly before ten o'clock the next day, Rufus and four other boys were picked up at the Happy Spot and brought to Cathedral Heights for questioning. It was now almost noon. In Sergeant Starkey's office, the air was acrid with tobacco smoke. A trusty in faded denim pants and shirt came through, emptying ashtrays into a gallon can. A radio in the interrogation room was playing softly, "You Dropped in for Tea." Here a jaded-looking plain-clothes man sat nursing a barnacled cup of coffee and keeping an eye on the boys sitting on a bench near the commander's desk.

The Moors had been grilled individually and collectively regarding a reported gang fight and case of arson, but apparently had been unable to contribute any information. Sergeant Starkey had angrily left his desk fifteen minutes ago. Rufus wondered what he was up to. The door opened again. Sergeant Starkey, in shirt sleeves, came in at a forceful stride. He carried a brown paper bag under one arm. Carefully, he placed the bag on the desk. Then he sat down and thoughtfully massaged his jaw.

Something told Rufus there was trouble inside that bag.

"I called your sponsor," said the sergeant. "He'll be along pretty soon."

"Thanks," Rufus muttered.

"You ought to have that cut stitched up, Willie," the officer said. "It looks real mean."

"It's okay," said Willie, touching a gash in his eyebrow.

"How did it happen?"

"I was taking a tire off a car and, uh—the lug wrench slipped."

"Oh, I see. Were you other boys changing tires, too?"

They grinned and moved embarrassedly, their eyes on the floor.

A young man in an ill-fitting suit entered and scrutinized the Moors. He had a country look. His fair hair was cut too long for a butch, too short for anything else. He might have wandered in off the street looking for Travelers' Aid—but a revolver bulged under his coat.

What goes on? Rufus wondered. He was growing apprehensive.

The commander leaned back in his chair. "You've got a real passion for wrecking cars, haven't you, Rufus?" he said.

"Don't know what you mean, Sergeant," the boy said politely.

"Guess. Guess what I mean."

"Tha. car I went to Pine Valley for?"

"That's one. The other is Simon Jones's modified Sherman Tank."

"I told you, Sergeant," Rufus said earnestly. "We were on the Big Lawn last night. Didn't you send a man over to ask Pelican Smith? Because he was with us most of the time."

The simple-looking officer spoke. "I just talked to Pelican, Rufus. For some reason he decided to lie, too. He says he was with you. You've got a real talent, boy. Anybody who can con Pelican into risking a jail term when there's nothing in it for him has got to be good."

Rufus relaxed. He heard the Moors stirring. All of them were incredulous that Pelican had decided to do what he had refused to do the other night. Rufus grinned boyishly.

"I don't know what made you think I was lying, anyway," he said confidently.

"You don't, eh?" The sergeant drew a length of green plastic hose from the bag. Without warning, he smashed it down on his desk. Everyone jumped, including the plain-clothes man.

"This!" he said. *"This* makes me think you're lying, Henry!" He drew another piece of hose from the bag and again struck the desk. "And this! Sergeant Roberts found these in a trash barrel at Gibson's while he was ranging around just now."

Baby leaned forward. "They looks like pieces of garden hose."

The sergeant smiled and spread his hands. "That's all they are, Gibson. Just pieces of hose. With sand packed inside them so you can fracture a man's skull with one blow! Practically everybody has them in his trash can."

The boys grinned, all except Rufus, whose mouth hardened as he thought: *Idiots! They packed the hoses after I told them not to!*

The door opened, and Alex Robbins came into the room, looking as neat and imperturbable as ever in his sharp, dark suit. But there was a grimness in the line of his jaw as he studied Rufus.

"Keep an eye on these citizens," Sergeant Starkey told the younger officer.

With a sense of frustration, Rufus watched the

commander lead the social worker to another office down the hall.

Sitting on the corner of a desk, Starkey waved Alex to a chair. Alex thanked him, but remained standing.

"Well, now, we've got a little problem," said the sergeant. He told the worker what facts the police had been able to put together. "The payoff," he concluded, "is that Jones is now trying to borrow a gun from the Pharaohs. Sergeant Roberts just picked the story up from the girl friend of one of the Pharaohs. Roberts is my gang liaison man, the young fellow outside. How do you people handle a situation like this?" he asked. "With a beach party?"

"If it were the Moors with the gun," Alex said, "I'd try to talk them out of it. Have you quizzed the Gassers about the fight?"

"Sure. But they won't talk. One boy has a broken collarbone. A kid named Shankman is being treated for possible concussion. But soon as Jones gets his breath, he's going to hit back—hard."

"Was there any cutting?" Alex asked.

"No. For once."

"And no real mean weapons used? I mean like chains and knives?"

The sergeant pondered. "I see. You figure the Moors were only having a little harmless fun."

"Not exactly. A piece of hose packed with sand can be lethal. But somebody seems to have gone out of his way to avoid bloodshed."

Starkey's cynical smile came. "Maybe somebody was afraid of going back to Pine Valley."

"If he was, that's progress. The ability to see farther than the next fight is a big step."

"Maybe if Henry'd started a year ago, he wouldn't

be under the gun, now. But he is. What's the book say the well-informed social worker does next?"

Alex creased his brow. He was accustomed to finding footholds where none existed. This time, however, he was dangling perilously by a frayed line. He knew so little about Rufus; yet his only hope of controlling the gang was through him.

"If we got these kids together on neutral ground," he began, "we just might slow them down."

"I hope I'm out of gunshot when we do."

"I've got a friend who's a trainer for the Marauders football team. I've already promised the boys to take them out to the team's training camp. Suppose we broaden the plan to include the Gassers? The boys would be too impressed to fight. It would be a chance to rub shoulders in controlled surroundings. And—well, you never know," he said. "It might be a start."

Starkey ruminated. "I'll go for anything, at this point. But how do I ship fifteen apes out there with nothing but one paddy wagon?"

"I'll send over two station wagons. There's an auto agency that loans us cars when we need them. You're not holding anyone, then?"

"I would if I could—believe me! But I have no evidence and not even a complaining witness."

Suddenly the officer went silent, cocking his head toward a snooper radio under the desk as it rasped: "—*Seven L Twenty, an ambulance cutting.*" He seemed to debate whether the call might involve juveniles.

"Okay," he said abruptly, "let's try it. I'll pass it along to Jones that the outing's coming up. Ernie Brown's a big hero with all these colored boys, of course."

Walking back to where the Moors waited, Alex reflected that the sergeant just didn't know the force of hero worship until he saw a scrapbook such as Parole Officer Travers had told him of. In a sense, it was unhealthy. Brown had become a god to Rufus. But that very adulation might be used to slow the boy down. It was that, as much as anything, that had convinced him the gamble was worth the risk.

He told the Moors: "The sergeant says you can leave now. There'll be a special meeting at seven tonight."

TWENTY-ONE

The playground was dark when the Moors arrived in two automobiles twenty minutes before the scheduled time. Idell was driving his brother-in-law's three-quarter-ton pickup truck. They stood at the gate suspiciously studying the cluttered darkness. In the shadows, the leaky drinking fountain dripped. Rufus's nerves twanged. Something about the darkness was wrong tonight. . . .

Then he saw a cigarette glow under a pepper tree. "Back in the cars!" he whispered. But just then they heard giggling.

"Hey!" a girl's voice called. "Are you guys the Moors?"

"That's us, beautiful," Rufus called.

"How you know I'm beautiful? Can't even see me."

"Just takin' a gamble," Rufus said.

"Come here," the girl called.

"Huh-uh. You better come out here."

Two girls walked from the darkness and stood under the streetlight. The boys ringed the girls, looking them over voraciously. One was tall and pretty, with a smooth brown face and large eyes. She wore a red shift and sandals. The other was tiny and dark in a turquoise blouse and skirt that failed to meet in the middle by several inches. The tall girl said, "We hear you messed up the Gassers last night."

Whitey tucked his hands in his hip pockets. "Where you hear that?"

"Oh, it all over the Flats," said the small girl. "We seen the wreck, too."

"You kids live in Durango Projeck?" Baby asked.

"Uh-huh."

"I've seen you around."

The tall girl was looking at Rufus. She seemed calm and self-possessed, but the hands that held her small plastic purse were clenched nervously.

"You're Rufus Henry, ain't you?"

"That is correct," Rufus said. "How'd you know?"

" 'Cause I've seen all the other guys here," the girl said. "I'm Judy Williams."

"Hi, Judy," Rufus said.

"This is my cousin, Nonie Emrey."

Rufus nodded to the smaller girl. He was pleasant but cool. Girls figured in his plans for the Moors, but not yet. He had been invited to parties by girls who, just for excitement, also invited members of a rival gang. The Moors were not ready for special situations like that.

"It nice meeting you," Nonie said to Rufus, with a big smile.

"What you kids want?" Rufus asked bluntly.

"We've got a club," Judy said. "Thought maybe you'd like to have a ladies' auxiliary, like the Gassers

has. They've got this girls' club called the Gasser-
ettes."

"I know. They're pigs," Idell said.

"They sure is," Nonie agreed.

"But they're a big help to the boys," Judy pointed
out. "They carries the Gassers' weapons when they're
going to throw. An' cops can't search a girl. So the
girls keep walking till the boys need the weapons."

"And that's what you want to do for us?" asked Rufus.

"That jus' up to you. We could give parties for you
and things."

"We were talking to Miss Dunbar, at El Sereno
playground, about giving a dance," Nonie added.

The boys made pleased sounds, but no one spoke.
They all glanced cautiously at Rufus. Up the street,
Rufus heard an automobile approaching. Old Alex!
Right on time to make them look like Boy Scouts
with a scoutmaster. He shook his head impatiently.

"Maybe sometime. We got a lot of work ahead of
us first. See you around."

He turned his back. Alex was parking his car behind Idell's truck. Nonie laughed nastily.

"Oh, we knows about Mr. Robbins, Rufus. We
wants him to sponsor our club, too."

"That's fine. Tell him about it sometime. You better take off now."

But the social worker was already approaching.
Seeing the girls, he smiled.

"Good evening, ladies."

With poor grace, Rufus made the introductions. He
tried to get the girls moving, but Judy blurted:

"We wants to hang around and listen to the meeting, Mr. Robbins. Maybe we'll get you to sponsor our
club, too."

"I'm sorry, girls," Alex said. "This isn't ladies'

night. If you really want a sponsor, though, I'll speak to my supervisor."

Nonie grinned. "We calls the club the Am-Moors," she said. "It Judy's idea. She got it out of a book. Ammour mean love, in French."

"Come on," Judy said quickly.

She took Nonie's hand and they walked away.

In the crafts room, Rufus sat on the long masonite table, swinging one leg and staring out the door. The boys roamed the floor, talking about the girls. They were exhilarated with success and relief. They had set the Gassers down and got off clean. Everyone within fifty blocks knew that Simon was a pedestrian now and that the Moors had become as hot as a seven-dollar pistol.

Deadpan, Alex watched them strut. His silence began to trouble Rufus.

"So what's new, Friend?" he asked.

"Simon Jones with a gun. That's new."

Baby took a chair. "Far as guns goes," he bragged, "there's a couple we can pick up too if we needs them."

There was a murmur of support. The Moors regarded Alex amusedly, sensing his dilemma. He wanted to castigate them for raiding the Gassers; he was dying to preach the Christian path. But he knew that if he so much as shook a finger at them, they would walk out. Rufus read this in their cocky grins. Yet he knew they had not begun to understand Alex. They thought they had him pegged, but he might still be holding a whole sleeve full of cards, and the big one was probably a badge.

"I think you'll agree, though," Alex replied, "that a shooting war would open a new phase in your feud. On the other hand, if the Gassers don't start shooting in the next day or two, they'll probably cool it and go back to conventional weapons. How do you fellows feel about an outing?" he asked.

Rufus blinked. "What kinda outing?"

"I told you I have this friend with the Marauders—Smiley Weber. I called Smiley today and got the green light for us to visit their training camp and meet Ernie Brown."

Rufus felt his stomach drop. Chairs creaked as the boys reacted.

"When's this gonna be?" Whitey asked.

"Tuesday afternoon. That would give you time to get ready. What do you say?"

"We ready now!"

Alex raised his brows. "Everybody got clean clothes?"

"Clean clothes!" Idell jeered. "Who are these cats —the Twelve Apostles?"

"Dress any way you want," Alex said. "Only, I should think you'd want to build your rep by being the best-looking group these men have ever seen. T-shirts, jeans, and tennis shoes ought to do it. You won't want coats, because you might get a chance to work out."

The group glanced at Rufus. "That's right," he said.

"I ain't got any tennis shoes," Everett said.

"I ain't got a T-shirt," said Idell. "I got a black shirt with long sleeves, though."

"Maybe you've got a beanie with a propeller, too," Rufus suggested. "Anything but T-shirts looks freakish on a ballfield. We'll have to raise some bread to buy the stuff we need."

"How?" someone demanded.

"How about a car-wash?" Alex came in quickly. "We'll put up a notice that on Sunday we'll be washing cars for fifty cents apiece in a Project parking lot. I'll bring the hoses, sponges, and chamois. You fellows bring the elbow grease, and the customers bring the bread."

"What's all this got to do with the Gassers?" Rufus asked suddenly, realizing Alex was pulling some kind of social worker snow job.

Alex explained about his conversation with Sergeant Starkey. A brittle silence fell. The boys were all displeased. Idell gnawed a fingernail.

"Huh-uh!" he muttered. "If they in, we're out."

Rufus frowned at the door. Idell was right: no good could come of confronting the Heights gang now. On the other hand, the thought of meeting Ernie Brown drew him powerfully.

"Take a vote, Leeroy," he said. "How many want the Gassers included out?"

The vote was unanimous.

"On the other hand," Alex suggested, "everybody in the Flats will know it's your party. By inviting them, you prove you aren't afraid of them."

"We already voted them out," Whitey retorted.

Alex stood up. "So you did. But you voted yourselves out, too. I can't be bothered arranging things unless it's going to keep the lid on."

Rufus looked at Idell, and sniffed.

"Talks just like a cop," he said. "But he's right about it proving we aren't afraid of them. What have we got to lose?" He shrugged. "Let's vote again. I'd really like to see those cats work out."

Leeroy asked for hands. The vote was still unanimous, but it was *for*, this time.

TWENTY-TWO

Rocky Acres was in the foothills east of the city. The layout reminded Rufus of the Pine Valley Honor Camp. There were barracks-style dormitories, a mess hall, and a field enclosed by a board fence to keep rival scouts from observing the Marauders' workouts. A special policeman waved the two station wagons that had transported the Moors onto the track surrounding the field. The gridiron was brown and beaten-down, with flimsy goalposts and blurred yard lines. Scattered over the field were players wearing faded red practice uniforms.

Alex parked before the spidery gray bleachers. In the sharp country sunlight, the Moors' new T-shirts were bone-white, their glistening faces all shades of tan, copper, and mahogany. Tight-lipped, Rufus watched the players on the field.

Which one's Ernie? he wondered.

"Man, they the biggest!" Idell muttered.

There was one player on the field who weighed over three hundred pounds; several weighed over two-fifty. When two men charged past after a loose ball, the ground trembled under Rufus's feet. But none of the men looked like Ernie Brown.

Baby Gibson demanded loudly, "Which one's Ernie?"

Across the field, a player in a white sweatshirt and

red pants looked around. His arm was cocked to hurl a pass. Instead, he shot the ball flat and hard across the field toward the Moors. Rufus broke from the line and made a jumping catch. The player clapped his hands together and came jogging across the field to meet them.

"That's him," Alex said, smiling. "The guy with the good hearing."

As Alex introduced the boys, Rufus stood turning the ball over and over, dumbly reading the words stamped into the leather. Ernie came along shaking hands. Rufus was obscurely angry—angry that a rich old ox like Ernie, a man who would desert his family, should have such a power over him.

". . . And this is Rufus Henry," Alex announced.

A large pink palm was extended to Rufus. Panting with nervousness, he looked up. The player was huge, a thick-walled fortress of muscle and bone. His jaws were wide, his rugged features a dusty tobacco brown.

"Hello, Rufus," Ernie Brown said. "Good catch, there."

Rufus heard himself blurting: "How come you're passing, man? You're too big for a quarterback. You haven't got the speed, or—or anything."

Ernie's face became stern, and he took the football from Rufus's hands. "Oh, I'm not so bad as all that," he said.

Rufus could scarcely speak for the commotion in him. "No, I—well, what I mean—if you're a half-back, how come you're wasting time practicing passes?"

"Oh!" Ernie said, understanding. "Rufus, the way this game is going, a halfback's got to be able to do more than run. Last season most of us tried a few passes. This season—well, I figure a halfback will soon be a kind of heavy quarterback, that's all." He slapped Rufus's shoulder. "Spot pass on the forty-yard hashmark!"

Rufus took off, long-legged and easy. His shoulders rolling loosely, he traveled; yards from the mark, he glanced over his shoulder. There it came! slamming home so close over his right shoulder that he had to twist aside to give it clearance, while his clawing hands reached.

Thud!

He took the ball just as he passed over the white line. Tears came to his eyes. It was so perfect. *If I told them he's my old man,* he thought, *they'd call me a liar.* But there it was: they even looked alike, down to the small ears like a spittin' cat's ears laid back.

As he rejoined the group, Ernie said: "Of course, it's harder to get accuracy with a three-hundred-pound lineman on top of you.—Gibson," he said, "get downfield."

Baby charged downfield and reached up, but the ball bounced out of his hands. Idell, Whitey, and Willie ran out, the others in turn. They missed their passes and fumbled the ball all over the field before they got hold of it. It had always seemed odd, to Rufus, that a kid who was gutty and mean in an alley fight could be as clumsy as a girl in sports. But the fact was, they were all fumbling and self-conscious, frightened of anything unfamiliar.

Two more cars rolled through the gate. Horns honked. Kids were yelling inside the cars. The Gassers had arrived.

Rufus watched them shake hands with Ernie Brown. Several other players came over. Most of the boys had bruises on their faces, and Dukie carried

one arm in a sling. But what made them all look odd
was that they were dressed for the street, not for football. Simon wore a long yellow car coat. Shankman,
the lanky stakeout man, wore a black shirt, black
jeans, and a black sawtooth hat.

Sergeant Roberts, the pink-cheeked plain-clothes
man, was with them, and another officer in a dark
snappy suit who was smoking a cigar. Both men
looked edgy. Whenever a boy would drift a couple of
feet from the group, the officers' eyes would bird-dog
him.

The Gassers did not look at the Moors, but the
Moors stood grinning at the Gassers until Alex
frowned and shook his head. A short, stout Negro in
a T-shirt and baggy pants came from the shower room
with a carton in his arms. He was Smiley Weber,
Alex's trainer-friend.

"How about some sandwiches?" he asked.

The Moors welcomed the idea, beginning to loosen
up. Alex went over and laid his hand on Simon's
shoulder. The yellow-faced boy regarded him icily.

"Simon, we've got a lot of sandwiches here. Somebody's got to help us eat them. How about bringing
your group over to the bleachers?"

Simon led his gang toward the bleachers. Sitting on
the splintery seats, the boys watched the Marauders
return to the field. Rufus's eyes never left Ernie
Brown. After a while Ernie came up and sat in the
neutral zone between the two gangs. He wiped his
sweating face on a towel.

"Any of you boys play football?" he asked.

"Yeah, Rufus played," Simon called, leering. "He
was waterboy of the Pine Valley third string."

"Ain't you learned yet to keep your mouth shut?"
Idell yelled, coming to his feet.

Alex's hand clamped on his arm. Idell sat down.

"I could tell you'd played, Rufus," Ernie said. "Where do you go to school?"

"I went to Lincoln last year."

"He's going to Camarillo State next fall," Simon jeered. Camarillo was a mental institution.

Sergeant Wenzle, the plain-clothes man with the cigar, said angrily: "Will you shut your mouth, Jones? We're going to have a good time here, and you'd better straighten up and fly right!"

"Yes, sir," Simon said. "Fly right. Yes, sir."

The Gassers chuckled. The police officers scowled.

"We don't want to keep you all day, Ernie," Alex said. "You probably want to get your shower."

"That's all right." Ernie seemed reluctant to let things end on a downbeat. And perhaps because he was a man whose own problems were eased in action, he said:

"Come on down to the field. I want to show you kids some things before you go."

The boys streamed down the bleachers, leaping from seat to seat. At Alex's suggestion, the Gassers peeled off their bizarre coats and hats. Coatless, they looked like plucked peacocks, exposed in all their meatlessness. Skinny, dark arms thrust from ragged shirt sleeves. They moved around uneasily, ducking their heads. Ernie deployed the Gassers on the goal line, the Moors twenty yards out. "I'm going to show you how to field a kick," he said. "Just catch whatever comes to you."

A punter downfield sent kick after kick booming toward them. Missed balls were bouncing all over. Ernie drifted around, showing the boys how to latch onto the ball without losing it. The kids tried earnestly and missed them all. But they were having fun, and Rufus thought about the Big Lawn and the games they could have, if things were different.

Now the punter pointed at Simon, in the center of the line. "This one's for you!"

Rufus watched Simon chew his lip and clench his fists. There was the *boom!* of the kick. The ball travelled slowly, a floater. It was going to fall exactly where the kicker had said. The red-haired boy back-pedaled, then changed his mind and ran forward. Then he saw his mistake and tried to back up at full speed. He tripped and sprawled on his back. The ball fell behind him.

The Moors' loud laughter rang. Willie blew a jeering shave-and-a-haircut on his harmonica that made Ernie laugh too. Even a few Gassers grinned. Ernie motioned to the Moors and led them back to the goal line to join the other group.

"Let me show you what you did wrong, Simon."

The boys grouped around him as he demonstrated how to catch the ball. "The easiest way is to 'cover it in'—catch it against your chest.—Rufus, let's see how they taught you to do it at Lincoln."

Rufus took his stance. "That's good," Ernie said. He put his hand between his shoulder blades. "But get set, solid. Always figure there's some bull about to clobber you the minute you've got the ball."

Rufus nodded. His heart turned with pleasure and gratification.

Simon's mouth twisted, his eyes rattlesnake-mean. "Don't get too close to him, Ernie," he warned. "I hear he's in love with you. Sergeant Roberts says he got a whole scrapbook of pitchers of you. Calls it his dream-book. . . ."

"Jones, shut—!" Sergeant Wenzle bawled.

Rufus charged Simon, but Shankman blocked him with a swing to the ear. They fell together and came up slugging. Alex, Ernie, and the police officers pulled them apart and separated the two groups, lecturing angrily. Rufus stared at Simon, embarrassed and wrathful. The Gassers' headman grinned back at him. Ernie took an arm of each and brought them together.

"There's no sense *atall* in you fellows carrying on like this! If you've got all that energy to waste, take up something constructive. Don't go around smashing each other like animals."

"Why not let 'em put on the gloves, if they want to settle something?" Sergeant Wenzle suggested.

"I'm not sure it would settle anything, Sergeant," Alex said quickly.

Ernie clapped his hands together. "I've got a big idea," he said. "What are you doing Thursday, Alex?"

"Nothing I can't put off."

"Why don't we get together at the housing project and talk about setting up a sandlot league?"

A stir went through the boys.

"Crazy," Alex said, smiling.

"Maybe I could get over once in a while and give the boys some pointers. Some of the other kids in the area might want to get into it, too.—How about it?" he asked Simon.

Simon spat. "How you men feel about it?" he asked his group, negligently.

"Well, man, I don't know," Shankman said, shifting his weight. "I don't know if we wants to get tied up like all that."

Ernie picked up a football and shoved it at Simon. "Take this along. Maybe it'll help you make up your minds. What I'm thinking about is a league in each of your areas. You'd be the charter teams. Later on you might be ready for interleague games."

"I'll tell you what," Alex said. "Let's all meet on the Big Lawn Thursday at one o'clock and talk it over."

"If something else don't come up," Simon said.

"Rufus?" Alex asked.

"Not much point in us coming," Rufus said, dryly "Us not having a football."

Ernie slapped him on the back. "Pick one up on your way out," he said. "I'll see you all Thursday."

TWENTY-THREE

Rufus drifted into the kitchen while his mother was preparing dinner. "Need any help?" he asked.

Mrs. Henry laughed. "How much it going to cost me, boy? This sound mighty suspicious."

She let him finish grating carrots for a salad, while Janet set the table. Curtis came in, and they all talked except Rufus. There was a good feeling, and Mrs. Henry told them about her day.

"Miz Fitzgerald goan to have a catered party next week. I tole her I got a big boy what could wash her windows for a dollar an hour, and she say that be all right."

"Okay," Rufus said. "By the way, I saw Ernie Brown today."

"On whose TV?"

"In person," Rufus said.

"He plays a trumpet, doesn't he?" Janet asked.

"Naw, he plays football," Curtis jeered. "He's a big-shot player. The biggest."

Rufus kept his eye on his mother, who had not turned from the stove.

"How come, Rufus?" asked Janet. "Was he at the playground?"

"Alex took us out to their training camp."

"Rufus, Curtis—go wash up," their mother said hastily.

"Ernie's coming over to help us organize some football teams," Rufus persisted. "How about that?"

"That's real nice.—I think I'll go borrow some coffee from Miz Walters." Mrs. Henry hurried from the kitchen.

Rufus gazed after her, perplexed. She was mighty slippery where Big Ernie was concerned. But before long he was going to pin her down.

Rufus secured permission from the Project manager to use the area south of the Project office for the rally. He sent Whitey and Idell out to spread word that Ernie Brown would be in Durango Project Thursday afternoon. On Thursday, the Moors gathered at his house and he looked them over. Everyone looked fairly sharp.

"You'd better pick me up at twelve thirty," he told Whitey. "We'll all go over together."

"I seen the Gassers last night," Willie mentioned.

"Where at?"

"At the Fat Boy's. My old lady took me up to the clinic about my earache. They all setting on a bench. And listen! They wearing black pants like Simon's and striped T-shirts!"

The boys laughed.

"That ain't all, either," Willie said pointedly. "Seems like Simon's aiming to get square with us today."

"Who says?"

"Girl I know up there."

"Did she go over to the clinic, too?" Rufus asked.

Willie grinned guiltily. "That was just a joke, about my ear. I used to live up there. Thought I'd drop around last night and see what the talk was. Don't know what Simon's got in mind, but this girl say he got plans."

Rufus gazed at him sharply. "Anything else on your mind?"

Willie scratched his neck and peered guilelessly into Rufus's eyes. "That scrapbook of yours, Rufe. What's it all about?"

The rest of the boys were listening with solemn interest. "It's a thing I kept when I was a kid," Rufus replied evasively.

"Can we see it?" Willie asked, his eyes innocent.

"What for?"

"I jus' like to know more about Ernie."

Rufus leaned forward. "Willie, man, you're going to find out more about Rufus pretty quick. That scrapbook is something I feel kinda funny about. It's like your old Mouseketeers hat, you know? It may look silly now, but when you were little you prob'ly wore it when you went to bed."

The boys chuckled, embarrassed. Willie winked at Idell, and dropped the matter. Rufus realized that Simon may have seriously tarnished his reputation by spilling it about the scrapbook. There was something freakish about such a scrapbook, kids felt.

"If that's all you got to say," he said coldly, "take off. I'll see you there."

By the time the Moors arrived at the Project, a crowd had collected on the Big Lawn under the new-leafed sycamores. Fifty or sixty boys stirred in small groups. A number of adults watched from doorways and windows. In an unmarked police car, Sergeant

Wenzle sat with his partner, smoking a cigar. An ice-cream truck pulled up and began selling ice-cream bars.

Rufus saw the Gassers under a tree with Alex Robbins, and felt a flick of displeasure. He could do without Alex as long as anybody; but if he were their sponsor, he shouldn't be hanging in with Jones's mob. He noticed too that Simon Jones was absent.

Alex strolled over, smiling broadly. "I'd like to have the hotdog concession on this affair," he said.

"How comes Jones isn't here?" Rufus asked.

"Shankman says he had a date with his parole officer. He'll be along."

Alex bought ice-cream bars for the Moors. While they were eating, a long coupe parked behind the police car, and Ernie Brown stepped out carrying a football under his arm.

There were yells of recognition. The loosely scattered crowd coalesced, encircling him before he could move. Small children jumped up and down before him. Adults crowded around to shake his hand. He looked like an amiable Hercules in slacks and sport shirt. Seeing Alex and the boys, he waved, but for the time being he was trapped.

Sergeant Wenzle pushed through the crowd, which parted magically at the smell of the law. He handed Ernie a notebook. "How about an autograph, Ernie?" he said.

Ernie wrote something for him, and an unscheduled autograph party was on. As the crowd grew, Ernie scribbled his name on paper bags, scraps of paper, and pages from Wenzle's notebook. Even the Gassers elbowed into the crowd.

Rufus missed Simon's arrival, but all at once he was in the midst of the crowd, shoving smaller children out of the way as he bulled his way toward the big man on the curb. He carried a wrinkled shopping bag under his arm.

"What's he got in that bag, you reckon?" Idell asked.

Rufus studied the redhead. "Probably their football—going to get it autographed." He was impressed with what a repulsive specimen the Gasser was. The laughing hyena of the Heights; a rabid hyena, however, whose bite could be fatal. He compared him with Ernie—clean, hard, every muscle tuned, always on top of the situation.

A cube of ice lodged in his belly.

What if I walked up right now and said, "Let's tell them about Leesburg, Mississippi, Ernie—" What could Ernie say?

Just leave it like that, maybe, not crowd him. *Let's tell them about Leesburg.* Let all these cats wonder what it meant. Then one day we come driving through the Project in his Cadillac, and he says, "This is my son, Rufus Brown. I'll bet you never guessed."

Simon reached Ernie and said something Rufus could not hear, then delved into the shopping bag. As he did so, he raised his voice.

"Got something here I'd like you to put your name on, Ernie. . . ."

As he pulled it from the bag, Rufus's belly suddenly iced up solid. In a glance, he knew it was his Big Ernie book.

Ernie accepted the scrapbook, seeming puzzled. He turned a few pages, closed it suddenly, and shoved it toward Simon.

"You'd better put that away," he said shortly.

"No—no! This here's a real special book, Ernie," Simon argued. "See here—inside the cover it say: '*My Big Ernie Book, Facks an' Pitchers collected by his son, Rufus H. Brown.' "*

Sergeant Roberts saw Rufus first. Though he had been sitting in the car, the sergeant was out and around it like a cat. He slashed over the lawn to tackle the running boy. Rufus smashed his clenched fist down on the young sergeant's head as they fell together.

There were shouts and gasps of surprise. Men were hauling Rufus up, and Wenzle's burlap tones warned that if anybody tried to get smart . . . !

They jammed Rufus in the back of the patrol car, with Ernie on one side and Alex on the other, both talking at once. Rufus continued to struggle. Sergeant Roberts thrust his head into the car.

"Say the word, Rufus! We'll put the arm on him for breaking and entering your house. It *is* your book, isn't it?"

Rufus stopped fighting, and shook his head. "Don't know anything about it," he muttered.

"Let's get in my car," Ernie said. "We'll cruise a while."

"Forget it!"

"Well, let me drive you home, at least."

Finally they persuaded Rufus to get into Ernie's car. They drove away, Rufus in back with Alex.

"I wish I could tell you how many times something like this has happened," Ernie said cheerfully. "Every boy has to have a hero. Often as not, it's an athlete."

"I'm sorry about that 'son' jazz," Rufus said. "I don't know who wrote it in there."

There was an awkward silence. He realized both men knew he was lying. "It's not important," Alex said. "All that matters is for you to realize that nothing Simon can do can really hurt you. He *had* to do something to square with you for wrecking his car—

assuming that you masterminded that little caper. Now he's had his inning. Let's pick another day for the football rally and start clean. Simon's not invited this time—not until we get his promise to behave."

Rufus stared up the street. "Stop past that dump truck," he told Ernie.

Ernie pulled up. Alex and Rufus got out. Ernie passed the scrapbook through the window. "I wish you'd keep this going for me," he said seriously. "Some day when they ask who Ernie Brown was, I'd like to be able to show them."

Rufus waved it away. "I'm getting kind of old for scrapbooks. That stuff about—about me being your son—I don't know; I was just horsing around one night pretending I was going to be an All-American or something, and—"

He shrugged and turned away. As he went up the walk, Alex called, "I'll drop around tonight, Rufus."

TWENTY-FOUR

That night Rufus would not leave his room for dinner. Finally Janet brought him a plate of food. "Rufus," she said, "don't feel bad. Simon's just stupid."

"How'd you know what happened?"

"Some kids were talking at the playground. Mr. Robbins is downstairs, now."

"What's he want?"

"He's talking to Mama about signing a complaint against Simon for robbery."

"You tell her to shut *up!*"

He closed the door and angrily attacked the food. He knew the worker had really come to ask about Big Ernie. The Head-shrinkers had finally got a rope around his scrapbook and put it in a cage.

Why don't you ask me about it, man? There's nothing to it. My old lady told me a whopper to stop me picking at her about my old man. She thought I'd take it for about three yards, but I grabbed it and went for a touchdown. Or maybe she knew I'd do it, he reflected. Maybe she thought it would shake me loose from the gangs—make me too proud for them. It made me proud, all right, but not that way. I carried Ernie like a pistol, for protection.

He turned out the light and listened to the freeway traffic until he fell asleep.

The next day he felt better; yet the big problem remained: What was he going to tell the Moors? He used to have a dream about finding himself naked in the schoolroom. Then he would wake up, dying of embarrassment, and find out—*wow!*—it had only been a dream.

But this time he was not dreaming.

All day he pondered how to deal with it. Somehow he had to let them know he was no different than before. Darkness came, and a flame lit in him. He felt unexpectedly strong and eager. The black panther stretching and coming out of its cave.

Trotting downstairs, he found Janet doing her homework in the kitchen.

"Where's Mama?" he asked.

"She had to go to the store. She's going to call on Mrs. Parks while she's out. Mrs. Parks lives in Escala Project."

"I'm cutting out for a couple of hours," Rufus said.

He pulled a drawer open, slipped a paring knife into his pocket, and walked out. At the Happy Spot, he found a half-dozen Moors talking with Judy and Nonie. The girls looked solemn, shy, and excited. Rufus flipped a quarter to Idell.

"Idell, man, get me a burger. Lots of mustard."

Idell's face sharpened momentarily, but he got up and went to the cookshack. Rufus took his seat.

"Well, man, how you feeling?" Whitey asked him.

"Well, great," Rufus said. "How's everybody?"

"Well, everybody's great," Whitey said, smiling nervously.

Rufus wished someone would ask about the scrapbook, so that he could make some explanation. He felt he had better play it cool by letting someone else mention it first. But no one mentioned it.

Suddenly Judy blurted, "The Harriet Beecher Stowe High School kids are renting a ballroom at a hotel for they graduation dance!"

"That is the biggest news since World War I," Idell said.

"They prob'ly gonna wear cocktail dresses and tuxedos," Nonie said wistfully.

"Wonder if I can still get into my old cocktail dress?" Rufus reflected.

Judy giggled. Encouraged, she touched his hand. "Hey, Rufus? Nonie and me wants to give a graduation dance, too!"

"Hoo-ee!" Whitey crowed. "What you graduatin' from—the Hall?"

"There ain't three of you girls even goes to school," Headshrinker piped.

"That don't keep us from giving a graduation dance, does it? The school kids will be graduating in three weeks. So why don't we give one? We'll ask anybody you wants us to."

Rufus wrinkled his nose. "Ask Starkey," he said. "He looks like a real smooth waltz type."

The other boys made similar suggestions, and the girls snapped back defensively. Suddenly Nonie turned to Rufus, her face bright with malice.

"You so smart, why don't you ask where Willie is tonight?"

Boom! Rufus thought. This is what they've been sitting on all day. He pushed his face into the girl's and asked, "Where *is* Willie tonight, woman?"

"He in the Heights."

"At the clinic about his earache?"

"No. At the Fat Boy's—talking to Simon Jones about joining the Gassers. He say he ashame' to belong to the Moors now!"

"Now, why would that be?"

Nonie bounced up with some smart remark on her lips, but Judy slapped her mouth and said, "You hush up! Rufus got the Flats right in his pocket. He got some trouble, maybe, but he know how to handle it. Ain't that so, Rufus?"

Rufus took the paring knife from his pocket and stropped it on his knee. "That's so if you say so," he said, smiling at Judy. He looked the Moors over reflectively. "I think Willie's asking to be beat out of the gang. What do you guys think?"

"That's what we think," Whitey said.

"Then why don't we go talk to Willie about it?"

Willie Clanton lived in a tattered green house on Fishman Street, near Durango Project. Shabby and scaling, it stood behind a tiny lawn of mowed weeds. A dead palm tree in the middle of the lawn had been sawed off, leaving a stub like a barrel. The stub had been hollowed out and geraniums planted in it.

The neighborhood was dark. The Moors lay in the shrubbery alongside the house, passing a bottle of vodka from hand to hand. Idell had brought the bottle. It was traditional to get slightly high before a ceremony like this. To Rufus's notion, the liquor tasted like a fairly good grade of gasoline.

It was past eleven o'clock when an old convertible came reeling down the street. It stopped before the house, and Willie got out. He waved; the car headed on down the street. As Willie started up the walk, someone whistled. There was a rustling of shrubbery. Willie halted. Someone was standing on the porch. It was Rufus. Willie took a stride backward, but hearing footsteps behind him, he stood still.

As Rufus came down the porch steps, Willie said feebly, "Hi there, Rufe."

"Hi there, Willie Boy. How you, man?" Rufus said.

"Jus'—jus' fine, Rufe," Willie said.

"That's good. I like my men to feel fine. You feeling fine on vodka or pills?"

"You name it!" Willie chuckled, stealing a glance over his shoulder. Baby and Headshrinker had now cut off his retreat. Other boys were sliding in from the sides.

"How's everything up in the Heights?" asked Rufus.

Without warning, Willie ducked and ran.

The boys let him pass, then pursued him silently as he raced up the street. There was only the slap-slap of tennis shoes to testify that life-or-death business was being transacted in the night. Letting Willie escape was part of Rufus's strategy. They could not beat him in front of his house without getting caught, but Willie could be counted on to run to a safe place —safe, at least, for them.

Willie cut down an alley and sprinted toward the freeway. He reached the maintenance road beside the big cement columns and scrambled up the fence. As he hit the ground, Rufus dropped inside the right-of-way and threw a tackle that brought Willie down in the deep, wet-smelling weeds.

Willie sat up fearfully as the Moors encircled him. "Whuh—whuh—whut's this all about?" he gasped.

"We heard you're joining the Gassers," Rufus said.

Willie's voice went high. "Now, where you hear that?"

"Level with me," Rufus said. "Do you figure the Moors are finished, Willie? So you'd better lash up with a fighting gang?"

"I swear, Rufe! Don't know what you're talking about!"

"Then maybe you'd better hike up to the ear clinic again, because you must be stone deaf."

As the Moors tightened their circle, Rufus remembered the night when he was beaten into the gang. But no one was going to interrupt them this time. No one was going to save Willie from the beating he had coming. The boys brandished rocks and sticks.

"They come for me," Willie said hopelessly.

"*Who* come for you?"

"Simon. I was heading for the Happy Spot last night, and they picked me up. That Simon—he running wild! He all over the Flats again, Rufe."

"How come they didn't whip you?"

" 'Cause they wants me for a spy."

Whitey clapped his hands. "Oh, now, listen! This cat gonna be wearing a *trench* coat if we ain't careful."

"It the truth! They knows I used to live up there, and they putting on the pressure that I got no right swingin' with a Flats gang. Like I'm a—a fink or something."

"Maybe they right," Whitey said, his eyes flinty.

"Get up, man," Idell sneered.

Willie gave Rufus a look of misery. Rufus felt a flush of shame. But he was the headman: the boys counted on him to enforce the gang's laws. Yet there was something else at stake that affected him as much as Willie. Every member he lost weakened his power by that much. If Willie went to the Gassers, Rufus had demonstrated that he could not hold his men.

Willie backed against a concrete arch, clenching his fists and dropping his head. Idell sparred for an opening. Headshrinker threw a rock. It was a small stone, but it opened a cut on Willie's forehead. He gave a grunt of pain, but held his ground. Watching him, Rufus wished it were one of the others who was being beaten out, for Willie had heart. Idell stabbed at his head; Willie ducked and jabbed back.

"Wait a minute," Rufus said hastily.

Idell glanced toward the fence. "Somebody coming?"

"No. I was just thinking—Willie, were you snowing us about Simon wanting you for a spy?"

Willie raised his right hand. "Simon swears to take you over! He say there won't be a Moors gang left when he's through. I'm supposed to tip him off next time you plan on throwing with them."

"And what did you tell him?"

Willie squirmed. "Well, man, look at it my way."

"I am. I don't like losing you, Willie, but I can't have finks in the gang. If I let you off, you've got to do something to show me you're worth the trouble."

The Moors began to complain:

"How come?"

"He asked for it, didn't he?"

When they quieted down, Rufus said: "It's time we set Simon down for good. I'm tired of horsing around with him. I want you to get us a rifle, Willie."

Willie shuddered, and the Moors went silent. "You gonna burn him?" Whitey asked, nervously.

"Willie can't buy no rifle," Baby said. "He's under age."

"All I'm askin' is, what you going to do with it?" Whitey persisted.

"I ain't stealing no guns, man!" Willie blurted.

"Then we'd better finish what we started," Rufus replied.

"Wait a minute," Willie said, hastily, pulling a dirty handkerchief from his pocket. He wiped the cut on his forehead. "If you really want a gun, maybe there's a way. You guys seen that cat named Goldie lately?"

"He still around," Idell said. "But he don't sell guns. Not that I knows of. I sells him a transistor radio now and then."

Willie told Rufus that Goldie delivered bundles of newspapers in a truck to corner newsboys. His side-line was buying stolen radios for three dollars apiece.

"Maybe he'd buy us a gun," he said. "Any adult can buy one. Walk in a surplus store and take your pick. Old U.S. army guns. Jap guns. German Lugers."

"And Goldie's going to do this for us?" White scoffed.

"He is if I tell him I'm going to the cops about him." Willie smiled.

Rufus began to nod. "That's good."

"What kind of gun you want?"

"A rifle. I'll give you till day after tomorrow. And tell him to bring ammo, too."

"What are you going to do with this piece, Rufe?" Willie asked curiously.

Rufus winked. "Oh, I'll think of something. It won't just lay around."

A light was burning in the kitchen when he returned home. His mother, in her best dress, was drinking coffee alone. She looked mysteriously self-satisfied.

"You just getting home from Mrs. Parks'?" Rufus asked.

"No, I just told the chii'ren that. I been to a meeting with Mr. Robbins's parents' group."

Rufus leaned against the doorjamb. "You out of your mind?"

"They really a very nice group of people," said Mrs. Henry. "I 'specially liked Mrs. Clanton."

"Willie's old lady?"

"Her. Mr. Robbins quite a card. He put us all at ease real quick, and two or three folks talked about the troubles they has with their kids. He say things going to get better."

Rufus snorted. "He'll have you all playing ping-pong in the Police Athletic League next meeting. Lots of luck, old lady!"

TWENTY-FIVE

The following evening Rufus went to the taco stand to wait for Willie Clanton. A half-dozen Moors were there, looking extremely dubious about the whole affair. He knew they thought Willie had taken him in;

that Willie had talked his way out of a beating with a lie. They were not even sure, probably, that he had any real use for the rifle. It might be a bluff to regain lost face.

It was an hour and a half before Willie showed up. He came to the table carrying a cup of coffee, and sat beside Rufus.

"Okay," he said.

"Where is it?"

"Under the freeway."

"What kind of gun?"

"German army gun. Goldie says if I put the bite on him again, it'll be the last thing I ever does. Says he can have me killed for ten dollars, going rate."

"If he kills you, Willie," Rufus said, "we'll kill him —free."

"Now, that's a real comfort," said Willie.

Rufus picked Whitey and Baby to go with him and Willie to inspect the gun. They climbed the freeway fence, and Willie led them to a spot in the tall weeds. The gun was wrapped in some yellowed newspapers. Rufus held it in his hands. It felt solid and heavy, and the barrel was short. Willie opened a box and handed him a cartridge. The fat shell tapered to a small steel-jacketed slug. Rufus opened the rifle breech and tried to insert the shell, but it jammed. He thrust his finger into the bore to see what was blocking it. A sharp flange creased his skin. He lowered the gun and looked at Willie, tight-lipped.

"Whose idea was this?"

Willie swallowed. "What's wrong?"

"The barrel's been messed up so it won't take a cartridge!"

"That fink!" Willie groaned.

Rufus shoved the gun at him. "Tell Goldie we want one that works."

"I go to shop tomorrow, Rufe—every Saturday. And he don't drop papers on Sunday. I'll catch him next week."

Rufus examined the gun again, and glanced up. He winked at Whitey. "How about that? He takes machine shop, huh? Must have all kinds of tools in shop—"

Willie shivered. "Man, I couldn't no more smuggle that cannon into shop—"

"Take off the barrel and wrap it up."

"An' what if the shop teacher asks what I'm doing?"

"Tell him you found it in a dump. You're fixing up a toy gun for your little brother."

Whitey kicked a rock in the weeds. "You ain't told us what we're going to do with this cannon," he said to Rufus.

"We're going to take turns being the Mystery Sniper," Rufus said. "I'm going up on that building across from the Fat Boy's some night and shoot a couple of holes in that old teakettle Simon's driving now. Then I'll hang the gun in an air vent and they'll never find it. In a few days one of you guys will lob a shell through a window of his house. We could keep it going all winter. 'Mystery Sniper Strikes Again!' It'll begin to look like it's bad luck just to know him."

Willie shook his head. "Man, I *hope* it's a mystery."

"Don't worry about a thing," Rufus said. "Simon's going to think he's taken on the whole U.S. army. See you tomorrow night at Baby's. We'll hide it in a ventilator up there till I'm ready."

TWENTY-SIX

Idell brought a bottle of Sneaky Pete wine and a fifth of vodka to the roof of Baby's Project apartment the next night. Waiting for Willie, they passed the bottles around. There were muffled laughter and horseplay. Rufus sprawled on his back squinting up at the stars. The liquor he had drunk buzzed in his head; his lips felt numb.

Idell flopped beside him in the gravel and asked, "How's that Mystery Sniper routine go again?"

They all moved nearer to listen. He said they would have to map the Heights and plan everything very carefully. They would hide the gun in airshafts, ventilators, and beneath houses. Each time they made a strike, it would be important to create a diversionary disturbance nearby. This would slow down pursuit and confuse the police.

"Like say we throw gasoline in every trash barrel in the block," he explained. "Just before I shoot the gun, you guys will set fire to the barrels. There'll be fire trucks and police cars everywhere—but no Moors. We'll be on the Big Lawn."

Chuckling, the boys lay on their stomachs and listened to him tell the story. A fine, fuzzy feeling suffused him. His head felt warm, and the building seemed to rock slightly. Someone handed him a bottle and he drank more of the cheap sweet wine. He kept talking.

It was boastful, confident talk, and the Moors were as drunk on it as they were on wine.

"One time when I was in the Cobras," he said, "the Sultans cut up one of our boys. We got bottles and rags and made Molotov cocktails. Our headman got a gun, and we took their beat apart alley by alley! They were a car club, and we set two of the cars on fire."

Huddling closer, the Moors listened raptly. Other stories came to his mind, but something slowed him down. It began to remind him of telling ghost stories around a campfire.

"And you got off clean?" Whitey prompted.

Actually, the Cobras' headman had gone to vocational school, and two others had drawn forestry camp. Rufus had run faster and got away, that time.

"Yeah, I got off clean," he said.

"How about when you stole that car and shot out streetlights?" Baby urged.

Rufus waved his arm. "That was nothing," he said.

"No, go on. Tell it."

Rufus took another drink to trap the good feeling that was fast slipping away, and told them how he and the Quarters had stolen a car across town and driven along shooting out streetlights with a zip-gun.

"We wound up shooting out six plate-glass windows in a downtown department store!"

"That was a swinging night, huh?" Whitey said. "How'd you come out of that one?"

Baby punched Rufus's shoulder. "Tell 'em!"

"I went to Pine Valley," Rufus muttered. "That's where I met Baby."

They laughed, as though it were the perfect ending for a big evening. "They racked you up 'at time, huh?" Somberness descended on Rufus like a blanket. They had as much chance of not getting caught in this Mystery Sniper attack as they did of jumping off the building without breaking their necks. Yet if you could not strike back at a repulsive alley cat like Jones, then how could you respect yourself? It was time to move against the Gassers. He had to lead or quit.

Hearing a sound, he raised his head. "Is that Willie coming?"

Whitey crawled to the stairs. "Soun's like his heel-taps."

"This gonna be great," Idell chuckled. "Them lousy Gassers be afraid to show theirselves onna street."

Rufus frowned at him. Idell sounded drunker than he had seemed.

It was Willie, but he carried nothing. They watched as he came over and sat down among them. He shuddered.

"Holy tomato!" he said.

"What's amatter?"

"I hid the damn' thing in the alley behind the shop. When I went out to get it, it was gone!"

Rufus sat up. His vision was unpleasantly fuzzy. "Willie, if you're snowing me—"

Willie explained the whole thing again, in more detail. "That the truth, man! It musta been stolen. Somebody han' me a bottle."

Rufus lay back. Secretly, he was relieved. He listened to the Moors accusing Willie of lying; of having sold the gun; of working for Simon Jones. At last he said, "Forget it. I'll think of something else."

"When?" Idell challenged. "Next winter?"

"We've got to make them come to us, like the other time," Rufus said. "That's the only way."

"They already come. They made a' ass out of you," Idell retorted.

Rufus raised his head and stared at him, and Idell mumbled something and hurled some gravel over the fence. Rufus sank back. He seemed to hear Alex's mellow laughter nearby, as though he were leaning against the fence, enjoying the Moors' predicament.

Fight Two grows out of Fight One, he had said. *Fight Three grows out of Fight Two—*

He was a great missionary. The kind that took all your weapons away and turned you loose to be eaten up by the animals. For all he had succeeded in doing for Rufus Henry was to make him realize that you could not win.

"How we going to bring them to us?" Whitey demanded. "They ain't going to fall for that same trick again."

"Who's got the vodka?" Idell growled. Someone passed him the bottle, but it was empty. He cursed and threw it aside. "Less go down to the Chinaman's and get a bottle."

"He won't sell you liquor," Rufus said.

"I ain't talking about buying it. I'll hook a bottle while you guys tip over his garbage can in the alley."

They put on dark glasses and trailed downstairs, moving heavily. There was a legend that if people could not see your bloodshot eyes, they would not realize you were drunk. *Not much!* Rufus thought ironically. A drunk announced himself like a neon sign. He hoped to divert them, for although they were drunk enough to find trouble, they were too drunk to be able to handle it.

They cut across the lawn to Durango. Four abreast they spread over the sidewalk like a scrimmage line. Pedestrians stepped from the curb to let them pass. We're the Moors! their scowls said. Get in our way and we'll stomp you. Heads thrust forward, arms swinging. But when they set us down in the interrogation room at the police station, Rufus knew, we're no better than anybody else.

He stepped out ahead as they neared the Happy Spot. "Don't know about you," he said, "but I'm zonked. I'm going to get some food."

He took his place at the window. The boys stood on the corner, debating whether to follow. Idell wanted liquor more than food; he needed to keep that bonfire going in his head and frighten away the spooks of uncertainty. Rufus could hear them arguing. He knew he stood at the same crossroads Bantu must have reached sometime in his leadership of the gang. A gang had to be kept busy. Busy meant fighting. Eventually, that meant another entry on your rap sheet. So where did you stop? And where, for that matter, had he started? It was a breathless race he had been in as long as he could remember.

Whitey came slouching to the window. "Gimme some coffee," he told the cook. One by one, the others ordered food and they wandered back to their tables. Two girls were sitting at the rear table. Rufus looked at Judy and Nonie with a pained grin.

"If you girls keep hanging around," he said, "we're going to start charging you rent."

Judy popped her chewing gum at him. Nonie sipped a soft drink through a straw. Both girls watched solemnly as the boys filled two tables.

"Where were you?" asked Judy.

"Around," Rufus growled.

"You guys are drunk," Nonie declared.

"Why you say that?" asked Willie. "We just took a little antifreeze to loosen up our engines."

"You *smells* mighty loose," said Nonie.

The girls, Rufus saw, were going to be poor company tonight. That was one reason boys did not like girls hanging around: they got their feelings hurt over things other girls said, and cajoled you into fighting with the boy friends of the other girls in order to rectify the wrong. You got your scalp split open, and learned that it was actually your girls who had started the feud. Eating his sandwich, he wondered what they were going to try to con them into.

The Happy Spot resounded with gloom. The Moors' walk had spoiled their fine alcoholic glow, and the real Moors had begun to show through, moody and uneasy.

"What night's tonight?" Baby Gibson asked.

"Thursday," Nonie said. "You so drunk you don't know what day it is?"

"Shut up, woman," Baby said. "Ain't we got a meeting with Mr. Robbins tonight?"

Rufus thought a moment. "We're not going," he said. "I don't feel like another car-wash."

"Won't he turn you in?" Judy asked.

"Him? He'll just talk. Alex has got a Size Two brain and a Size Twelve mouth."

Judy moved closer to Rufus. With her forefinger, she began tracing a vein on the back of his hand. *Here it comes,* he thought.

"I worried that he'll turn you in, Rufus," she said.

He gave her a stare of cold amusement. "I'm worried about what you're working up to," he said.

Both girls began talking angrily at once, startling the Moors. "This here dance the Harriet Beecher Stowe High School kids are giving makes us sick!" Judy blurted. "They nailing posters up all over town! If I wasn't going to have no better band than four sophomores that calls themselves the Big Timers, I sure wouldn't advertise it."

"And all the talk they giving out about door prizes," Nonie sniffed. "Big prize!—a set of plastic hair curlers, prob'ly."

"Best favor they can do the public is to call it off," Judy said.

Rufus caught on, now. School was ending, graduation impended for seniors—but not for dropouts. When you were on a twelve-month vacation, mid-June meant only that in two weeks it would be July. The girls were jealous of their nondropout friends—that was all the fuss amounted to.

"We ought to give a dance of our own," Judy suggested timidly. "Call it the Moors' graduation dance. Maybe Mr. Robbins could get us a little hall somewheres. . . ."

The boys jeered. "Yeah—Juvenile Hall!" Idell laughed.

"Nonie and me got a whole lug-box of records," Judy persisted.

"When we wants music," Whitey said, "we drops a nickel in Willie."

"Drop a nickel in him now," Judy suggested.

Willie gave the harmonica a wipe for luck and began playing. Nonie and Judy danced together on the grease-stained bricks as the Moors clapped the beat.

"A dance sure would be fun. . . ." Judy said, yearningly, when Willie lowered the harmonica.

"All the kids in this end of town going to be at that dance," Nonie declared. "I don't see why we can't give our own."

The boys groaned. "Forget about it!" But Rufus seemed, all at once, to hear something like the wail of a jazz horn. The sound was purely in his head. He had a vision of boys and girls in their best clothing, dancing in some vague hall. The crowd was huge; posters tacked around the wall stated that the dance was being given by the Moors.

"Shoot," Leeroy said, "even if we gave a dance, the

Gassers would crash."

"Well, man," Baby said, "are you saying we can't handle them cats?"

"Let them come," Idell said. "We ready when they are."

The good feeling came rolling over Rufus again. He closed his eyes and let it sweep him up. It carried him high, like a breaking wave, and gave him the vision of a prophet. In his exaltation he knew he was ready, now. He would have to fake everybody—his own men as well as the Gassers. He must play it alone, so that when they carried those redheaded Heights cats out of the hall, even the police would not know what had happened.

He finished his coffee and threw the paper cup at a barrel. "Let's go over and see if old Alex is there," he said.

"I thought you weren't going," Judy said.

"I'm thinking about giving a dance," Rufus said. "I might feel him out on it. See if he'll help us." Judy squealed, and he scowled. "Don't start spinning your records, woman," he said. "I may do it, I may not."

"Okay, Rufus!" she said. "It all up to you." She looked at Nonie, and shivered with delight.

Rufus strolled to the sidewalk. In five minutes telephones would be ringing all over the Flats.

The Moors are giving a graduation dance!

Who's invited?

Where they holding it?

Let's crash it, huh?

Let's break the records and steal their women.

Come right in—help yourself, he thought. *But if any records are broken, the Moors will break them —the record for most Gassers laid out in one night.*

TWENTY-SEVEN

In the crafts room at Walnut Street playground, the gang sat around the masonite table. They were forty-five minutes late, but Alex Robbins had not mentioned it. All the boys wore sunglasses, and the place smelled like a barroom. Whitey chewed his lip and wrote down in the composition book Alex had given him what members were present. They had discussed the idea of a dance on the way over, and the boys were eager.

Rufus kept waiting for Alex to say something about the lost gun barrel. He was getting the feeling that the man had stool pigeons on every streetcorner. But nothing was said about it. Alex asked them how things were going, and they all mumbled, Fine, okay, everything's great.

"Okay, then, what's up?" asked the worker. He wore the amused expression of one who is a jump ahead of the opposition.

"We're thinking about giving a dance," Rufus said.

Alex blinked. "A dance? What kind of dance?"

"Graduation dance. Everybody else is graduating. Don't see why we can't throw a gig, too. We could make some bread out of it, and build our rep."

"How big a dance?"

"Two or three hundred kids."

The Moors made small sounds of wonder and excitement.

Alex tapped his pencil on the table. "I don't know whether you're aware of it," he said, "but graduation dances are pretty hard to control."

"Then we'll hire special cops."

"Cops cost money, Rufus."

Rufus scowled. "You don't get the picture, man. This is a *dollar-a-head* dance! Ties and coats. I'm gonna rent a dinner jacket, myself."

"I never been to a dance like that, Rufe!" Baby blurted.

"Not many kids have. That's why they're going to remember the Moors' dance. What do you think?" he asked Alex.

"I think you're biting off quite a lot. Finding a band might be hard—hiring a hall—getting posters printed . . ."

"We can do it in a week," Rufus boasted.

"Can you find a hall in a week?"

"What about the Club Chic?" asked Whitey. "It's an adult social club. They rent their hall on a split basis, so we wouldn't have to lay out no cash."

"Know anybody in the club you can talk to about it?" Alex asked.

"Mr. Bartell, the president. He run a record store on Durango."

The Moors chattered about renting dinner jackets, having their hair straightened, and clipping the guests by charging twenty cents for drinks. Rufus realized Alex was gazing steadily at him with eyes sharp with suspicion.

"Rufus, I've been conned by experts," said Alex. "And I have a feeling I'm being conned tonight. *I* think this dance is just a trap to square with Simon Jones."

Rufus looked at the others, as though baffled by such a thought. "How come a trap, man?"

Alex gave a sardonic laugh. "Come on, Rufus the Gassers have *got* to come to a dance as big as this, or everybody will say they're afraid of you. So what's to prevent your laying for them at the dance?"

"You just said we'd have special cops. That's what."

Alex toyed with his pencil, scrutinizing Rufus's face. "Mmm-hmm," he said, thoughtfully.

"I wouldn't snow you, Alex," Rufus pleaded.

"Not much," Alex said. He rubbed his nose. "However," he sighed, "if you fellows want to do the work, I'll sponsor the affair."

"You okay, daddy!" Idell yelled.

"Big hand for Mr. Robbins!" Rufus shouted, beginning to clap. The Moors applauded, while Alex smiled quietly until they were through.

"The snow's getting so deep in here," he said, "that we may have to dig our way out. Now, then, you've only got a little over two weeks. I'd suggest holding the affair the week before the regular graduation dances, so that the potential guests won't all be too broke to come."

The place began to jump. Everybody had an idea, and they were all yelling at once. Finally Alex quieted them. "If you're really sincere, I'll help all I can. You'll be high society if you pull it off. Half of Simon's own gang will be trying to join the Moors, because you'll be the guys that make things happen."

Rufus lay awake refining his ideas. He did not see how the bomb he was planting under Simon could fail to explode. Simon would wreck the dance all right: he *had* to. But the police would salt him down for so long afterward that people on the street would be calling him Uncle when he came back.

TWENTY-EIGHT

The Club Chic hall was up a long flight of stairs from Durango Street. Five days had passed since the talk with Alex. The boys had brought him over this morning to get his approval of the hall before they signed up for it.

"Have you got a firm date?" he asked as they climbed the stairs.

Rufus hesitated. "Mr. Bartell wants a fifty-dollar guarantee. We're trying to talk him out of it."

"Keep trying. Money is one thing I can't help you with."

At the top of the stairs was a plywood barrier with a ticket aperture and peephole cut into it. The barrier angled around to form a blank wall on the right. Alex nodded approvingly.

"Good arrangement. One officer can handle all the incoming traffic."

In a big, lobby-like room beyond, a dozen card tables were arranged on a scarred floor. The dingy room smelled of moth balls. Along the right wall ran a bar littered with artifacts of some previous party —empty soft-drink bottles, faded streamers of crepe paper, a girl's slipper.

"You could rent the tables for a couple of dollars each," Alex suggested.

"Good idea. We'll reserve some for ourselves and rent the rest."

Alex crossed the room to gaze over a low divider at the dance floor. At one end was a raised platform with a microphone stand. A streaked photomural of a big-city skyline covered the far wall. Alex turned, and seemed to be looking for something.

"Is there a telephone?" he asked.

Rufus led him back to a room above the street. With its blue walls and lack of furniture, it was empty and depressing. A wall telephone hung between two windows. A fire escape angled across them. Alex listened for the dial tone to be sure the instrument was connected.

"Nice to be able to send out for help in case of a brawl." He smiled. "You've only got ten days, now, so you'd better stir yourselves. How about the band?"

The boys looked at Rufus. "We thought we'd use records," he said.

"At a dollar-a-head dance? Your guests will expect a band, and yell till they get it! Call the musicians' union and ask for the name of a band leader. How about special policemen?" he asked.

Rufus rubbed his neck. He was becoming confused and vaguely panicky. The problems kept coming, like cars in a freight train.

"How much will they cost?" he asked.

"About fifteen dollars apiece. Do you want me to make the arrangements?"

"Okay. I'll try to line up a band."

He called the musicians' union later, and asked for the name of a band leader. The union secretary told him to look up a musician named Bill Dibbs, who had a small combo. The address he gave Rufus was in the downtown area. Rufus took Whitey along for moral support.

Bibbs's street was narrow and dirty, lined with pawnshops and honkytonk theaters. They entered a small hotel that looked a century old. In the middle of the lobby was a railed area like a bullpen where shirt-sleeved men loafed before a television set. A man told them Bibbs's room was on the fourth floor, and took them up in a grilled elevator like a bird cage.

Rufus knocked at the door. For some time there was no response.

At the third knock, bedsprings creaked and a man's voice called huskily, "Okay, man. Don't knock the do' down."

A thin, cigar-brown man wearing tuxedo pants and an undershirt let them in. He yawned as Rufus explained what they wanted.

"I wisht the union would tell people a musician's day don't start till two o'clock," he said. "One of you good lads run down and get me a cup of coffee, eh?"

Whitey ran off, and Rufus sat on the single chair. The room was small, with an enormously high ceiling and walls of cracked plaster. There was a small, dirty window. Rufus waited while Bibbs washed up. When Whitey arrived with the coffee, Bibbs drank some, and relaxed.

"Now, then," he said pleasantly.

Rufus told him they needed a small band for Saturday night, two weeks from tomorrow. "We can't pay a lot," he added, hopefully.

"I'd have to charge scale," Bibbs said. "A non-union band might play for less, but they're unreliable. Might promise to be there, and not show up."

"How much is scale?"

"Figuring for a four-man combo, ninety dollars."

Rufus winced. "How much for a three-piece band?"

"I wouldn't recommend less than four," Bibbs said

firmly. "What you might do is to hold your gig on Friday instead of Saturday. Scale is less. Cost you seventy instead of ninety."

"I guess Friday'd be okay," Rufus agreed.

Whitey stirred restlessly on the unmade bed. "Maybe we'd better give up," he said.

The room was silent. Rufus knew he had gone too far to turn back; that, actually, there was nothing to go back to.

Suddenly Whitey jumped up. "Thanks a lot, man," he muttered. At the door, he glanced back at Rufus and jerked his head. But Rufus remained seated.

"When would we have to pay you?" he asked the band leader.

"That night, before we start playing."

Rufus rose and tucked in his shirttail. He chewed a knuckle. "Seventy bucks, huh?"

"Best I can do."

Rufus told Bibbs where the dance hall was, signed a contract the musician produced, and they left.

Mr. Bartell would not budge a nickel's worth on his deposit requirements. It was fifty dollars, take it or leave it. The gang scoured the Flats for another hall, but there was nothing suitable.

Rufus went back to Mr. Bartell's record store and said, "How about it if we give you an extra ten after the dance?"

"The hall has to be cleaned, boy. Should I pay that out of my own pocket, and maybe you decide to call the affair off?"

"We won't call it off."

Mr. Bartell was a gray-haired, aristocratic-looking Negro with a sharp eye. He leaned on the counter and peered into Rufus's face. "You really want to give this dance?" he asked.

"Yes, sir."

"Enough to clean the hall yourselves, before and after?"

"Yes, sir!"

"Mop and wax the floors? Wash the windows? Dust everything?"

"Yes, *sir!*"

"All right. Two days before the dance, you come back and I'll show you where the cleaning things are."

Rufus hurried off to tell the Moors the news.

They met at the taco stand later and designed a poster. Then they took it to a printer, who said he would print a hundred posters in old-style type for twenty dollars.

The ink was still wet next day when they left the shop, each carrying a bundle of posters to place in store windows. Rufus took a bus to Cathedral Heights, got off near the Fat Boy's drive-in, and entered a barbershop. The barber agreed to let him put a poster in the window. As he set it up, Rufus studied Durango Street. There were no redheaded Negroes in sight, and he went out and walked to a grocery store, where he left another. He placed several more placards before a Flatsbound bus came along.

In an hour, Simon Jones would be reading a poster that advertised:

THE MOORS
INVITE YOU TO THEIR
GRADUATION DANCE!
Club Chic Hall   Admission One Dollar
First Twenty-five Girls Free!

On Thursday they cleaned the Club Chic hall. Mr. Bartell's wife managed to be on hand all day. Before night, the floors and windows sparkled. The boys' hands were pulpy from immersion in ammonia and hot water, and their nails were polished with floor wax.

Rufus stopped by Judy's apartment on the way home. Her hair was rolled up on huge pink curlers. "Pick you up tomorrow at seven," he said.

"Okay, Rufus. This sure going to be a wonderful evening!" She sighed.

Walking home, he felt a twinge of guilt. She had never had an evening like they were about to have, that was for sure!

TWENTY-NINE

Friday night Rufus bathed, shaved, and dressed. His starched shirt popped like sheet metal, and the studs would not stay in place. He went to the head of the stairs.

"Old lady? Come here!" he bawled. His mother hurried upstairs. "These fool studs keep coming out!"

"Getting mad won't help," soothed his mother. With pins, she secured the studs. She helped him on with his jacket, and he looked at himself in the bathroom mirror. He was pleased at what he saw. Black and white were just right for dark skin. Standing behind him, his mother patted his shoulder as though she were smoothing a wrinkle, but her hand lingered.

"Don't my boy look fine, though," she said, in a caressing tone he had not heard in years. Embarrassed, he shrugged her hand away. He did not like emotion, and he hated being touched. But something else was wrong, too; a fever that had been incubating in his mind for several days had suddenly broken out with the violence of a disease.

What was wrong was that this dance, which was essentially a self-destroying weapon like a hand grenade, had mysteriously come to life for him. There was certain to be a fight like World War III tonight. The thought of the Moors' big plans being wrecked made him sick. A tender, protective feeling, much like his affection toward Janet and Curtis, had developed in him where the dance was concerned.

"You all right, Rufus?" asked his mother. "You sweating."

"This shirt's like an oven," Rufus grumbled.

He checked his clothing once more, muttered, "Well, so long," and left the house.

Judy must have been watching for him, for as he turned up her walk she came hurrying to meet him. Rufus regarded her with pleasure. Her black cocktail-length dress flattered her figure; her shoes were pastel pink; and a pin sparkled in her hair. He told her she looked great, with the same surprised tone he might have used if she had appeared in a fur coat.

"Don't ack so surprised," she replied haughtily, taking his arm; but added, "You looks mighty nice yourself."

As they started off, an escort of noisy children skipped along beside them. The rest of the gang and their dates waited before the taco stand. Strung out two-by-two, they strolled to the Club Chic in the smoky city night.

The street door was unlocked, but at the top of the stairs, a husky officer in a white leather jacket blocked their way. Another man in a pale blue uniform stood nearby. Alex introduced the kids, then he looked them over approvingly. They stood pleased but self-conscious under his praise.

"We've still got a hundred folding chairs to set up," he told them. "A couple of you boys had better help Mr. Bartell, too."

The club president was working behind the bar with another man, lining up cases of soft drinks. Rufus and Baby removed their jackets. "One of you crack the ice in this here tub," Mr. Bartell said. "The other can set out paper cups."

At eight o'clock, Bill Bibbs and his band climbed the stairs, lugging instruments. They arranged chairs on the bandstand, tested the sound equipment, and settled down to joking with the girls and trying to bum cigarettes from everyone.

At eight-ten, Sergeant Roberts and Sergeant Wenzle arrived for a look around. They stood on chairs to search the air conditioning for weapons and liquor; they sniffed the entire hall like beagles, and finally frisked the boys.

"Is there going to be any trouble, now?" Wenzle asked Rufus, sternly.

"Not from us, Sergeant," Rufus said. His hands were numb from cracked ice, but the coldness was no greater than that in his stomach. As Wenzle turned away, he spoke quickly.

"Sergeant?" Wenzle turned back, quizzically. "Can I ask a favor?" Rufus said.

"Why, certainly," the sergeant said, looking surprised.

"Will you station somebody downstairs to keep the Gassers from crashing?"

Wenzle shook his head. "We can't tie up a car all evening, Rufus. Anyway, you've got these instant cops to keep the peace, haven't you?"

"They'll be needed on the floor. I mean somebody on the street to keep them from coming in at all. If they crash—well, you know what'll happen. . . ."

"Crash?" Wenzle chuckled. "You can't keep anybody out of a public dance, unless he's obviously drunk. You know what I think?" He gave Rufus a sly wink. "I think you've got a bad case of combat nerves!"

Helplessly, Rufus watched him stroll to the stairs and disappear from view.

Alex hurried over to where he was working a few minutes later. "Get your coat on!" he said hastily. "It's early, but there must be a hundred kids milling around in the street! There'll be a traffic problem on the stairs if we don't let them in."

The first couple paid their admission at the box office and wandered to the edge of the floor. Alex and one of the special officers searched the boy for bottles and weapons; then Alex gave him a congratulatory pat on the back and turned him loose. From their tables, the Moors and their dates watched the guests enter.

"Ain't that Pelican Smith?" Judy whispered.

Rufus regarded the boy. He was tall and high-shouldered, in a black suit with brass buttons. It was the youth he had talked to that night in Escala Court the headman of the Bloods.

"That's him. Hope he ain't coming to make trouble," Whitey said.

A nervous, gum-chewing girl clung to Pelican's arm. Pelican gave them a solemn nod as he strolled to another of the reserved tables.

Couples kept streaming in, dressed in the best clothing they owned. The empty hall filled. Before the initial run dwindled, over two hundred tickets had been sold. A few boys were sent home to get neckties. All the reserved tables were sold, and soft drinks were going at fifteen cents apiece. In the dim light, softened further by dust, the old hall looked fine. Tiny globes in the ceiling winked like stars.

"It's so quiet!" Nonie whispered.

The lack of noise and roughhousing puzzled them all. It seemed as though the guests were awed by the dollar's worth of magic they had bought. People were already glancing impatiently toward the bandstand; however, Bill Bibbs and his musicians lounged around as though this were their night off. Suddenly Rufus remembered the deal; no money, no music!

He rushed to the box office, where Mr. Bartell counted out seventy dollars and he signed a receipt. Then he handed the money to Bill Bibbs. The band immediately came to life. As Rufus returned to the table, the music started with an ear-splitting assault of brass.

Rufus and Judy struggled about the crowded floor. Dust and a blue ceiling light created a hazy undersea magic. The girl put her lips close to his ear.

"What's wrong, Rufus?"

"Nothing. Why?"

"You acts funny."

"I just dance funny."

The music died, and again the hall was eerily quiet. To Rufus, the silence seemed ominous. People wandered around with paper cups in their hands. Alex circulated unobtrusively, and even the special officers with their nightsticks managed to look almost like guests.

The music ripped loose once more with unnerving violence. They struggled back to the floor. A flute voice wailed eerily up and down. Sweat broke out on him. He felt trapped in the heat and airlessness of the throng. Biting his lip, he scanned the crowd for hostile faces. When the music finally expired, with a wail like a punctured tire, he wilted.

Pushed along by the crowd, they drifted back to their table. As they neared it, however, he sensed that something was wrong. Whitey and Nonie were standing beside the table with stiff and angry faces. Their chairs had already been taken. With a shock, Rufus recognized the two couples who had pre-empted the table.

Simon Jones, Shankman, and two girls with huge beehive hairdos were grouped around it.

THIRTY

Rufus walked to the table and stood beside Simon Jones. The gang leader smiled up at him, his lemon-yellow features cocky. "How's yo' father, Rufus Brown?" he asked. "Don't hear you talk much about ol' Ernie these days."

"You've got our table," Rufus snapped.

"You keeping that passing arm in good condition, Brown?" asked Shankman, his teeth shining in a grin.

"Good enough to throw you down the stairs if you don't move."

Simon frowned and made an impatient gesture. "Now, man, we paid our taxes. Go away. We having *such* a good time."

Rufus loomed over him with clenched fists, and Simon got up hastily. But suddenly one of the uniformed officers was standing beside them, swinging a nightstick and smiling.

"Everything all right, folks?" he asked.

Simon bobbed his head. "Just fine, Officer," he said, pleasantly. "Just real good."

"That's fine," said the officer. "Why don't you and your friends find chairs along the walls? This table is already taken."

Jones's group made elaborate apologies, and left. The officer winked at the Moors and strolled away. Judy glared indignantly after the Gassers.

"Make him throw them out, Rufus! They going to spoil everything, sooner or later."

Rufus sighed. "We can't throw them out until they do something."

The Gassers were the first dancers back on the floor, moving around like discus throwers and shouting back and forth. "Tell 'em, sister!" Simon shouted, as the vocalist started her number. A somber quiet settled upon the crowd. Some of the couples left the floor.

The music ended. Rufus led Judy back to the table. He searched the room for the Gassers. They had not resumed their seats along the wall. He found them, eventually, ranged along the west wall, near the box office. The girls were no longer with them. The boys were still roughhousing, pushing at each other and laughing, but their actions were forced. Rufus narrowed his eyes suspiciously.

Why had the girls left? What went on?

He noticed that the gang kept glancing surreptitiously at the wall behind the soft-drink bar. Scrutinizing it, he saw nothing but streaked plaster and a couple of grilled ventilators. But the police had searched the ventilators for weapons and liquor; so what was the big joke?

"They's a terrible smell in here," Nonie said petulantly.

"That's just Gasser stink," said Whitey, bitterly. "It does smell funny though, don't it?"

In fact, now that Rufus thought about it, he too had been noticing an odor. The Club Chic had begun to smell like Ace Tire & Retread—like cooking rubber. He turned to stare at the ventilators in the wall, and started. Heavy and black, smoke was pouring through the grilles into the room.

Rufus started to lurch to his feet. They all looked at him, puzzled. He sat down again and hunched over the table.

"Listen! There's either a smoke bomb in the heat system or else the buildings's on fire—"

Nonie opened her mouth to scream, but Rufus clapped his hand over her lips. *"Shut up!* It's probably just a smoke bomb. There's smoke coming out of the vents. That's what you smelled."

Judy began to cry. "I spent seven-fifty on my hair," she sobbed, "and I borrowed my married sister's dress, and—"

"Will you *shut up?"* Rufus said. "The Gassers are moving toward the stairs, so they must have done it. They'll be the first ones out when somebody yells, 'Fire!' "

He looked at Whitey hoping for a comment or suggestion. But Whitey was paralyzed with terror. He looked as though he had been dipped in hot wax. Helplessly, Rufus stared around the hall. Bill Bibbs was joking with some guests standing before the bandstand. As he noticed the microphone on its stand,

Rufus poked Whitey with his thumb.

"Go tell Bibbs to make an announcement!"

"You mean that—that there's a fire?"

"No! That there's no reason to get excited. It's just a short in the wiring, or something—"

Whitey got up and started for the dance floor.

Rufus studied the Gassers again. They were quieter now, but they had drifted closer to the .stairs. They stood against the wall, near the door to the coatroom. Rufus saw other guests wrinkling their noses and beginning to look around. When that first yell came, everyone in this hall would pile into that narrow stairway and clog it like steers in a stockyard chute.

He stood up. "You girls stay here. Don't try to leave, whatever happens. If people panic, those stairs will be bad news."

"Where you going?" Judy demanded fearfully.

"To find Alex."

To his relief, Alex was not far off. He, too, was trying to locate the source of the smell in the hall. Rufus waved and caught his attention. They met near the box office.

"Somebody planted a smoke bomb in the basement!" Rufus said. "Whitey's telling Bibbs to make an announcement."

"Good," Alex said. "I want you to go to the coatroom and phone the fire department. Then open the windows onto the fire escape, beside the phone."

Rufus gestured toward the Cathedral Heights youths. "You're going to stop those slobs, aren't you?"

"I'm going to try. If I can't, we'll pick them up later. The important thing is not to have any trouble. We can't risk a riot for the little satisfaction bagging those boys might give us."

He gave Rufus a push toward the coatroom. Rufus

moved. His path took him behind the gang. For a moment he hesitated. There were plenty of folding chairs at hand. It would be easy to swing one and drop a couple of the punks before they escaped. . . .

But the important thing, as Alex had said, was not to have any trouble. Rufus strode into the coatroom to the telephone.

A woman who sounded like a female robot answered his call. He gave her the information, and ducked out of the room. At the head of the stairs, Alex was trying to restrain the Gassers. Simon and two other youths were arguing with him and pushing him back toward the stairs. The loudspeakers crackled.

"Folks, are you having a good time?" Bill Bibbs's voice asked. There was some anemic applause. By now, nearly everyone was staring around the room, and a number were quietly heading for the exit. "Reason I ask, we hope you'll bear with us while we straighten out a situation in the basement. Seems like some practical joker has set fire to an old inner tube in the heat system! Now ain't that a panic? So there'll be a little smoke in here till the fire department pumps out the vents—"

Rufus saw Shankman throw a punch at Alex's head and try to run past him. The worker caught his arm, twisted it, and jammed the boy face-first into the wall. Rufus picked up a chair, swung it above his head, and rushed toward the redheads as they charged the stairs.

The boys halted just short of them, blocked by a man who now stood there with his hand on the shoulder of a redhaired Negro boy wearing horn-rimmed glasses. Rufus recognized the punk they called Dukie. The man was Sergeant Wenzle.

"I caught this character running down the alley,"

he said. "I thought I'd better bring him upstairs and see if there was any trouble."

"No real trouble," said the worker, cheerfully. "Just arson and conspiracy—some minor matters like that. Let's go in the coatroom and see what these boys have to say for themselves."

While the men herded the indignant youths through the door, Rufus felt his anger and strength leaking out the soles of his feet. Music swelled above the uneasy murmur of anxious guests. In a moment, everyone was on his feet. But most of them were moving toward the dance floor.

THIRTY-ONE

"I wish you could have been there," Alex Robbins told Rufus's mother. "You never saw a finer bunch of kids in your life."

They were drinking coffee at the short-legged kitchen table. Three days had passed since the dance. The rented tuxedoes had gone back to the shop, the lights were out at the Club Chic, and the Flats were the same dreary hole once again. The worker said he had dropped by to let them know that the Moors had cleared twenty-six dollars on the dance.

"I think that's real good," he said. "You fellows could buy a few days at summer camp for that kind of money."

Rufus was not especially pleased over the visit.

These cats were always trying to rush you off to the nearest Scoutmaster, just because you passed up a chance to get in trouble. But after a few minutes more, Alex thanked Mrs. Henry for the coffee and said he would have to be running along. Rufus was surprised. His mother, however, spoke to Alex before he could rise.

"I been thinking about school for Rufus next fall, Mr. Robbins. And I was wondering—"

"Whether he could get back in?" Alex suggested. "Well, I suppose he might have to go to a continuation school for a while. But I'm sure we could work it out."

Rufus scowled. "I went that continuation route, once," he said. "Guy came at me with a file, in shop. I had to cool him down with a mallet. And we *both* got expelled."

"There might be problems," the worker conceded. "But nothing worth while is ever easy. Isn't that so?"

Something in his smile as he rose, compelled Rufus to smile also. He shrugged and walked with him to the door. "That's so if you say so, Chief," he said.

ACKNOWLEDGMENTS

Without the generous help of George Nishi-naka, A.C.S.W., director of Special Service for Groups, a Los Angeles agency working with juvenile gangs, I should have been unable to explore the sad, boisterous, and often violent world of the youngsters whose stories I have tried to gather here into a single tale: that of Rufus Henry.

Through Mr. Nishi-naka's good offices, I was enabled to attend meetings of street club workers with their group; to visit camps and accompany gang members on outings; to be present at staff meetings and conferences of workers and a psychiatrist when behavioral problems were clarified; and to attend meetings of the parents of gang boys and girls with the workers. I was so impressed with the dedication and ability of the people I met at S.S.G. that I resolved to try to tell their story in the framework of a novel.

Rufus Henry, the hero of the story, is a Negro, and most of his friends and enemies are Negroes. It would be a mistake to conclude from this, however, that the members of any one race are more gang-oriented than another. All races contribute their share to the ranks of delinquent gangs. What does seem to be true, though, is that racial discrimination is a strong factor in the formation of such groups.

A gang is not merely a collection of juvenile delinquents. It is a group of very special delinquents whom the police, the playgrounds, the schools, and other agencies have been unable to help. Recognizing this, the police do not rate as a "gang" a group of youngsters who get together infrequently for the purpose of committing lawless acts. To qualify as a bona fide gang, delinquent youths must misbehave with specified regularity and in groups of a certain size.

To the gang boy or girl, the gang means protection against other such groups. But it also invites beatings by rivals, as well as attention from the authorities. A boy or girl who joins a gang, therefore, must have some good reason for doing so, though he may not be able to explain it. Perhaps it is his way of telling a world he feels unequal to that, while he may appear to be nobody, he is in reality a Copperhead, a Royal Aztec, a Mau Mau, or a Little Diamond—and people had better give him room when he comes down the walk.

Special Service for Groups attempts to break up such fighting gangs by assigning an experienced and resourceful social worker to a gang that has been having more than its share of trouble with the authorities. Often more than half of its members are on probation or parole. The worker's task is to learn the problems of the individual members and help solve them. He does not expect to be welcomed. Indeed, he knows that it may well be months before he is accepted, if he is able to penetrate the gang's defenses at all.

More often than not, however, he is finally successful—so successful that, when he tries to "terminate" the group after a year or two, he is scarcely able to free himself of the kids' desperate grasp on him. But termination must come, if they are ever to learn to go it alone, without a worker and without a gang.

Among the members of Mr. Nishi-naka's staff who helped me in my research were Alex Norman, Ellen Dunbar, Herk Biskar, and Herman Fogata. Special thanks are extended to Lily Shitara, who was helpful in leading me though the labyrinths of the agency's archives.

I should also like to acknowledge the co-operation of Capt. W. L. Richey, Juvenile Division commander, Los Angeles Police Department; Sergeant Nielsen, Juvenile Division; Sergeant Walter, Hollenbeck Division; and Jim McClellan, Newton Division, all of whom were helpful in defining the problems of the police officer trying to cope with the violence of a big city.

Alex Norman and Jim McClellan were kind enough to read the manuscript of the story for errors, not only from the standpoint of social workers of long experience, but of officers in civil rights groups.

F.B.

"Simply one of the best novels written for any age group this year."—*Newsweek*

I AM THE CHEESE

BY **ROBERT CORMIER**
AUTHOR OF <u>THE CHOCOLATE WAR</u>

Adam Farmer is a teenager on a suspenseful quest, at once an arduous journey by bicycle to find his father and a desperate investigation into the mysteries of the mind. What exactly is Adam looking for? Where is his father? Why does he have two birth certificates? What is the meaning of his parents' whispered conferences? Of their sudden move to a new town? Of his mother's secret Thursday afternoon phone calls? Of the strange man who appears and reappears in their lives? And why are Adam's thoughts constantly interrupted by an unidentified interrogator who prods him to recall some recent, devastating catastrophe? "The secret, revealed at the end, explodes like an H-bomb."—*Publishers Weekly*

LAUREL-LEAF BOOKS **Laurel-Leaf** $1.95

At your local bookstore or use this handy coupon for ordering: